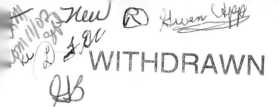

BABY IN A MILLION

BABY IN
A MILLION

BY
REBECCA WINTERS

MILLS & BOON®

First published in Great Britain 1998
Large Print edition 1998
Harlequin Mills & Boon Limited,
Eton House, 18-24 Paradise Road,
Richmond, Surrey TW9 1SR

© Rebecca Winters 1998

ISBN 0 263 15632 X

Set in Times Roman
16-9807-50868 C16½-18

Printed and bound in Great Britain
by Antony Rowe Ltd, Chippenham Wiltshire

CHAPTER ONE

WHEN the phone rang, Ashley McKnight got up clumsily from the kitchen table. She'd been folding clothes which had just come out of the dryer and hurried to answer it, afraid it might waken Mrs. Bromwell who had finally fallen asleep, hopefully until morning.

Though Ashley turned off the elderly woman's phone every night, the second extension in the kitchen lay on the other side of the wall of the comfortable apartment. Any noise past ten o'clock could disturb her because she suffered from crippling arthritis and the medicine didn't always blot out the pain. But she was such a dear soul, she hardly ever complained.

The only people who would phone her this late would be Mrs. Bromwell's family to see how their mother was doing, and how Ashley was faring. They had a replacement for Ashley, realizing that if she went into early

5

labor, she'd have to leave their mother on a moment's notice.

But her doctor expected her to go full term, which meant she had four more weeks until the baby was due—four weeks to earn a little more money. Besides needing to outfit a layette, she had attorney fees to pay. She'd signed the papers. Now it was Cord's turn to sign so that their divorce would be final right away.

Out of habit she lifted a hand to smooth the hair from her ear, still forgetting that she'd had the long, thick, molasses-colored mane cut off last month. Her new short, stylish wedge-cut felt cool and would be much easier to manage with the approach of the baby and the hot summer coming on.

"Hello?" she said quietly.

"*Ashley*—"

Her sudden intake of breath robbed her of speech. She hadn't heard that deep voice in eight months, hadn't seen her husband in all that time.

Since she'd sworn her attorney to secrecy, the only way Cord could have found out where she was living and working was through Greg Ferris, Cord's best friend, the owner of an exclusive sporting goods company in Salt Lake where she'd done a lot of the accounting until the time she'd left her husband.

She'd thought Greg was *her* best friend, too! He'd promised not to tell Cord where she lived, or that she was pregnant. That kind of news she intended to keep from her husband until after the baby was born and she had settled elsewhere.

After several years of trying to conceive, they'd gone in for tests and had found out Cord had a problem which made it almost impossible for them to have children.

When she'd left his house for good, it would never have occurred to her to think she was pregnant. Not only because of the medical reasons, but because the last, disastrous six months of their hurtful marriage had been spent in separate bedrooms.

From the first moment Ashley had been introduced to Sheila, Cord's stepmother, the other woman had made subtle remarks out of Cord's hearing which insinuated that she and Cord had enjoyed a romantic relationship before her marriage to his father—that they still desired each other.

Confused and appalled by the revelation, Ashley had tried to put the whole thing out of her mind. For the most part she had succeeded.

She and Cord couldn't travel down from the Teton Mountains of Wyoming to Salt Lake very often. As a park ranger, he didn't take that much time off from his work to get away. But when he could arrange it—mostly so they could visit Greg and his wife in Salt Lake— they only stopped off to see Cord's father and stepmother for short periods of time, whether it be at the office or at the house.

Somehow Sheila always managed to say something in private to Ashley which alluded to Sheila's past relationship with Cord. But it wasn't until the death of Cord's father that Sheila grew bolder and played on Ashley's doubts about Cord's interest in his stepmother.

As time went on, and Ashley's marriage to Cord began to disintegrate because of insurmountable problems, the doubts grew until Ashley feared that Sheila was telling the truth.

Only once, the night before Ashley had moved out of the house, had Cord come to her, trying to persuade her to believe in him, to stay with him, telling her that Sheila meant less than nothing to him, that it was Ashley he loved.

Like a fool she'd succumbed to that moment because it had been such a long time since they'd been together, and she was still so desperately in love with him.

When morning dawned and she found herself alone in the bed, she went to his room in search of him, wanting with all her heart to believe that he'd meant what he'd said.

Oh, she found him all right. Sheila was there, of course. Ashley's worst fears had been realized.

After a night of such incredible passion, the pain of his betrayal with his father's widow had torn her heart to pieces. In agony, Ashley had fled from him with her bags, never dreaming he'd made her pregnant.

If he knew she was carrying his child, he might delay the divorce, escalating attorney costs. He'd insist on taking care of her. *He'd be relentless*. It was something she wouldn't be able to tolerate, not when it was excruciatingly painful to be around him.

Just hearing his voice again set her heart thudding with sickening force. Well into the final stages, the pregnancy made her short-winded anyway. But to know that the man she'd loved to the exclusion of all else—despite everything she knew he'd done—was on the other end of the line, left her feeling faint and dry-mouthed.

"Hello, Cord."

Good heavens. She'd attempted to infuse a businesslike quality in her tone, but her voice betrayed a pathetic nervousness.

"It's nice to know you remember me," came the silky rejoinder.

Remember you? She tried to swallow her pain. Though separation had brought physical closure to the insoluble problems of their six-year marriage, part of her had never let him go. Even if she weren't pregnant with his child, she knew it would be impossible to get over him.

How many times had she relived the fantasy that one day the phone would ring, that it would be Cord calling her with proof that there'd never been an affair with Sheila, that it had all been a mistake... That he still loved her, Ashley, and wanted her back.

But this was no fantasy phone call. His sarcasm crushed her. Eight months of separation hadn't changed anything. One bitter remark from him and they were back in battle mode, as if they'd never been apart.

All they managed to do was hurt each other.

Her hand tightened on the receiver. "If you're not calling me to let me know you've signed the divorce papers, then I don't know why you bothered."

She hadn't meant to sound so curt, but it was her only defense against the old emotions swamping her. Though he hadn't asked for a divorce, she knew he'd wanted one so he and his father's predatory widow—the woman who was now a voting member on the board of the McKnight Company—could be together.

To accommodate him, Ashley had filed. That was the pain she lived with day and night.

"I'm fine. Thanks for asking," he mocked with bitter irony.

She couldn't take much more. "I—Is there a point to this conversation? I'm very busy and it's late."

By now her voice held a distinct tremor. No doubt he'd heard it. She couldn't bear for him to know how much this phone call had shaken her.

"Actually, there is."

"If you read the papers my attorney sent your attorney, this couldn't possibly be about money. I never wanted yours, and I'm making an adequate living."

The quiet on the other end of the phone let her know she'd said the one thing guaranteed to anger Cord. It had infuriated him that she didn't want alimony. She heard his sharp intake of breath. "This has nothing to do with money."

Ashley bit her lip. *Was he about to tell her he knew she was pregnant*?

If Greg hadn't confided that information to Cord, then she couldn't imagine what this was all about unless he'd heard she *was* hard-pressed for money.

Only because she'd been given room and board to be a companion and do light housekeeping for Mrs. Bromwell, did she have a decent place to stay. The family of the feeble eighty-year-old woman who never left the house paid Ashley a small salary which she was hoarding for the time when she had to find another place to live and work after the baby was born.

Soon she would move into the vacant tiny one room basement apartment around the corner to get things ready for the baby.

Though it was the last thing she wanted to do, she'd probably have to sell her diamond ring to help pay for the delivery. The proceeds from the sale, plus the little money she'd saved would keep her afloat until the baby had come and she could look for another caretaking position that allowed an infant.

"I've a favor to ask," came his deep-toned, vibrant voice over the wires.

Favor?

Her delicately arched brows drew together in a frown. After trampling all over her heart until he'd ground it to pieces, he wanted something *more* from her?

"So if I don't grant it, you won't sign the papers? Is that it?"

"One has nothing to do with the other. I'm waiting to hear from my attorney."

How did he maintain such perfect control when she was on the verge of hysteria?

"I think I'm the wrong woman to ask," she bit out at last. Her whole body was trembling. "What could you possibly want from me now?"

The question was out before she realized how angry she sounded. *And how vulnerable. Damn, damn, damn.*

"You're the one who ended things by moving out on me—" his voice grated "—but that's all past history. What I'm asking for is a little of your time."

His calm reply enflamed her.

"Ask Sheila."

There was another deadly quiet. "Aside from the fact that she has nothing to do with my personal life, you're the only person who can help me. I'm calling from City Creek Hospital," he added quietly.

As a dozen ghastly scenarios flashed through her mind, she suddenly felt sick to the pit of her stomach. "What's wrong?" She almost strangled on the words.

"It's not fatal," he answered in a dry tone, obviously reading her mind with his usual accuracy. His explanation released the tight band around her chest, allowing her to breathe again. "But I'd rather discuss it with you in person."

"No!" she cried out in fright. Since he was still in the dark about her pregnancy, she didn't want him to find out about it yet.

Rising to her feet in a panic she said, "If this isn't a life-and-death situation, then there's no reason why we can't talk on th—"

"As I was about to say," he broke in civilly before she'd finished, "you have every right to refuse me."

Cord had a way of baiting her which not only pushed every button, but managed to make her feel sorry for him so she ended up battling a large dose of guilt for something she hadn't even done. Flushed because of the late stage of her pregnancy, their conversation had raised her temperature another couple of degrees.

"To be honest, I'm surprised you haven't already hung up on me."

She held her forehead in her head. He would never beg. It wasn't his way. So why had he called? What was really going on with him?

"Cord—I fail to see—"

"The *point*?" he interrupted once more. "I suppose I should have expected that response from you. Rest assured I won't bother you again."

Beneath his wintry delivery, there was a bleakness in his response which haunted her long after the line had gone dead...

When Ashley went to bed a half hour later, she tossed and turned all night. The pain in her lower back, coupled with the activity in her womb would have made her restless anyway, but Cord's phone call had disturbed her so much, she knew she wouldn't sleep until she knew the real reason why he'd contacted her.

They were getting divorced. Their marriage was over. Soon he and Sheila could do whatever they wanted without interference. It was nothing to do with Ashley, not anymore.

But he had phoned with a specific purpose in mind. Maybe he'd been diagnosed with something terminal, but not immediate.

No matter what had happened to break them up, the thought of him no longer existing on the planet brought pure terror to her heart.

The next morning, after she'd prepared Mrs. Bromwell's breakfast, Ashley left her listening to a book on tape. With a small grocery list in hand she took the car to the store, then drove to Greg's office located on the east bench, ten miles from the apartment. If anyone knew the truth, he did.

''Hi, Sally,'' she said to one of the clerks on her way back to Greg's office where she used to work. Now that spring had come to Utah, the store was packed with people already dreaming about summer campouts, ready to take advantage of the sales on new tents and lanterns.

Seconds later she gave a little rap on the door to his suite, their private signal.

Greg looked up with a broad smile and leaped out of his chair. ''My, my how you've blossomed since I last saw you. You look beautiful.'' He gave her an affectionate hug before telling her to sit down opposite his desk.

Happily married to Bonnie, and the proud father of two adorable children, Greg had been her rock and confidant when things had started to go wrong in her marriage to Cord.

She didn't want to believe that he would have betrayed the trust she'd placed in him. If he'd gone against her pleas not to tell Cord anything, then she needed to know about it right now.

If he'd kept his promise, she needed to know that, too, so she wouldn't be angry at him for something of which he was ignorant.

"What brings you here unless it's to get your old job back? Much as I like Elly, she's never been able to fill your shoes. She doesn't understand the business the way you do. Everyone around here still misses you like crazy."

"Thanks, Greg. That's nice to hear."

"I'll tell you what. If you'd reconsider working for me again, I'll buy you a reclining chair, and we can put a cot in back room when you need to lie down." He kept it up with that winning smile. It warmed her aching heart.

"Greg—you're wonderful, and I treasure those words, but you know why I could never come back here to work."

His expression sobered and he leaned forward in his swivel chair. "Cord doesn't come in the store anymore if that's what you're worried about. If I want to talk to him, I have to do the calling. Even then, he's not himself. The last three times I've asked him to go spring skiing with me, he's turned me down. Frankly, I'm worried about him.''

The fact that Cord had called her from the hospital made what Greg said that much more alarming.

Evidently their impending divorce had caused a breach in Greg's relationship with Cord, something Ashley wouldn't have imagined happening. They'd been friends for years and loved each other like brothers. The two couples had been on dozens of weekend vacations together in the mountains.

If he'd closed up on Greg, then she had to assume Cord's problems had to do with Sheila. When the divorce was final, Ashley didn't suppose he could contemplate marrying his father's second wife without alienating a lot of people, but it would be Greg's opinion that mattered most.

Since Greg had done everything in his power to help them fight for their marriage, she could only assume Cord was staying away from his closest friend to avoid talking about the past or being made to feel guilty.

She took a shuddering breath. "Did you by any chance give him my phone number?"

Greg's eyes narrowed. "Did he phone you?"

"Yes. From City Creek Hospital. Last night."

"*Thank God*!"

Ashley was taken back by such heartfelt emotion. "Then you told him where he could reach me?" she asked incredulously.

"Yesterday morning," he said with a nod. "I had to, Ashley. Cord is in serious trouble."

A spurt of adrenaline made her feel dizzy. "He said it wasn't fatal."

"He was lying!" he fired back. "I'm convinced you're his only lifeline. Have you seen him?"

"No," she said on a ragged breath. "I'm afraid our conversation degenerated rather quickly. He insisted on seeing me in person. I told him no and he hung up." Her voice trailed.

She heard an unintelligible epithet come out of him. He sounded so much like Cord just then, it stunned her.

"Did you tell him I'm pregnant?"

"No. He has no idea he's about to become a father, nor does he know where you live, or how you're earning a living. Since you refuse to go to him, I guess that's it."

For the first time since she'd known Greg, he was making her feel guilty. "Do you know what's wrong with him?"

He grimaced and it aged his appearance. "I have a gut feeling, but it's not my place to say." His amber eyes stared directly into hers. "You really have cut him completely out of your life, haven't you?"

"Greg—" she defended, "if Bonnie had ever done to you what Cord and Sheila—"

"Ashley—" he broke in not unkindly, "I didn't say that to hurt you. I suppose I was hoping time might have softened the wounds, but apparently I was wrong. I love you and Cord, and can see that both of you are in horrendous pain. It's hard to sit back and do nothing, but that's exactly what I've done all this time up until yesterday when I went to see him. That's when I felt I had to intervene."

Ashley started to feel physically ill and couldn't talk for a minute.

"I'm sorry you've lost confidence in me, Ashley, but I won't apologize for wanting to help save him. One thing I can promise you, he'll never try phoning you again. Seeing how bitter you still are, it took more courage on his part than I would have had to reach out to you one last time. To be completely honest, I'm shocked he actually had the fortitude to make contact."

He was sounding an awfully lot like Cord.

"Am I such a horrible person?" she finally asked in a dull voice, dying a thousands deaths inside.

"You know better than to ask a question like that. I'm not judging you, Ashley. I'm not in your shoes and couldn't possibly presume to feel what you're feeling. All I know is, two wonderful people who seemed so perfect for each other are now living drastically altered lives and I'm helpless to do anything about it."

Ashley couldn't take any more. "Greg— I didn't mean to place you in this terrible position. I don't blame you for what you've done." Her voice trembled. "In fact I love you for caring so much. I don't want to be a bitter woman. There's nothing uglier or more self-destructive.'' She lifted her head and eyed him levelly. ''D-do you know his room number at the hospital?''

''He's not in there now.''

''What do you mean?''

''When you didn't come, he checked himself out and went home.''

''*What*?'' With difficulty, she got up from the chair. ''But that doesn't make sense.''

''I guess it does to him.''

She bit her lip. ''I—I'll phone him as soon as I get home.''

A somber expression darkened his features as he rose to his feet and walked her to the door. ''Please, Ashley,'' he whispered against her forehead where he gave her a kiss. ''Don't do anything unless you mean it.''

Don't do anything unless you mean it?

Those words went 'round and 'round in her head all the way back to the apartment.

As soon as she'd put away groceries and prepared Mrs. Bromwell's lunch, she left her propped up with pillows listening to the radio, then shut the door and reached for the phone. But fear of becoming vulnerable again prevented her from actually punching in the numbers.

Another hour went by while she debated what to do, all the while growing more and more frantic. Finally, when she couldn't stand it any longer, she picked up the receiver and phoned Cord's extension at the office. Most of the time Sheila answered it for him.

Prepared to hear the satisfied sound in her husky voice, Ashley was taken aback when a terse, ''Yes—'' came over the wire to meet her ear. He had to be in a vile mood.

''Cord?''

For once the deafening quiet coming from his end told her she'd caught him off guard.

''*Ashley*? *Dear God*—it *is* you.''

The raw emotion in his voice revealed that she still had the power to affect him in some small degree. Summoning her courage she said, ''I went to see Greg today. He said you'd left the hospital. Why?''

''Does it matter?'' he asked grimly. ''Last night you said you didn't want to hear anything I had to say.''

She was afraid it would be like this. "Cord—do you want me to go on, or shall we just hang up?"

"No. Don't do that! I've been in a foul mood and didn't mean to take it out on you."

If she didn't know better, she would say he was nervous, which was odd because Cord wasn't the nervous type. Anything but. At least she could say that about the Cord she thought she knew. Right now she didn't know anything anymore.

"If you need to be in the hospital, then I don't understand why you went back home. What's wrong with you?"

"It's my worry, Ashley. I'll deal with it."

She frowned. Something was missing in Cord, some elemental spark which had always been there before. She couldn't put her finger on it, but the fact that he didn't seem like himself bothered her terribly. Especially when he was going to be a father soon.

"I've made a decision, Cord. Please check yourself back in and I'll come over."

"Because of problems at the office, I couldn't go in before Monday. But in any case, it's asking too much of you."

Greg had intimated Cord was deeply depressed. She was starting to realize what he'd meant.

"Not according to Greg," she interjected. "He seems to believe you're in real trouble."

"He's exaggerating."

"I don't think so. Let me know when you're back in City Creek Hospital and I'll be there."

"No, thanks. Your sacrifice isn't required, certainly not this close to the divorce. I should never have called you. I'll work on my problem in my own way."

Ashley felt a stabbing pain in her heart. He sounded like he was giving up. She couldn't let this go, no matter the situation with Sheila.

"I—I'm afraid it's not just your problem any more."

Another long silence ensued. "What in the hell do you mean by that?"

At least she'd roused him out of his morose state for a moment. "All will be explained when we see each other Monday morning. I'll be there early."

Without giving him a chance to respond, she quietly put the receiver back on the hook. Only now was it hitting her what she'd done.

Because she had agreed to meet him at the hospital, he would find out she was practically ready to deliver their child.

Not only would he be hurt and angry that she hadn't told him, he'd be in shock. According to the tests, their pregnancy had to have made medical history.

She had a premonition that once he found out, everything would grow more complicated and the divorce would be prolonged. But she'd taken the risk and couldn't go back on her word now. Not if something was really wrong with Cord, and she firmly believed there was.

Without wasting another moment, she called the Bromwell family to arrange for someone else to come in to watch after their mother.

On Saturday, when Mrs. Bromwell's oldest daughter came over to the apartment with the new person hired, Ashley went shopping for some new maternity clothes. She couldn't spend much money, but she needed a few decent outfits to wear to the hospital. In the end, she bought several pairs of tailored cotton pants and artist's smock tops in a flowered print, plus a couple of dresses.

At five after six Monday morning, Ashley stepped through the doors of the hospital and walked over to the main desk. "I'm Mrs. McKnight. Has my husband, Cord McKnight, checked in yet?"

The receptionist typed in something on the keyboard and scanned the screen. "Yes. He's here. Room 521-C. Take the east elevators to the fifth floor, then turn right and report to the nursing station. They'll direct you from there."

"Thank you," she murmured with a sigh of relief. All weekend she'd worried that Cord wouldn't show up after all.

With trepidation and a heart that was hammering out of control, Ashley headed for her destination. By the time she entered the elevator with her suitcase and sewing bag, she felt jittery and uncertain.

In the last eight months she'd become a different person physically. Though more slender than ever in body and limb, she was pregnant enough to look like she could have her baby anytime now.

Many women with their first pregnancy didn't show as much as she did, but that was probably because she was five feet four and there was no room for her baby to grow but out. No wonder Greg had commented on how much she'd blossomed when she'd visited him on Friday.

As she made her way down the hall, she wondered if Cord would even recognize her, especially with her short hair. Friends and acquaintances who'd known her when it had been long said they liked it both ways. But they thought the pixie style showed off the smooth oval of her face and brought out her slightly almond-shaped eyes which were a mixture of blue and green. Cord had always remarked on how they shimmered between her dark lashes whenever she was in the throes of deep emotion.

She'd debated over wearing her wedding rings, but at the last minute decided she'd better keep them on. She and Cord were still married in the eyes of the law, and she had an idea Cord wouldn't like it if she didn't show up with them. Better not upset him any more than necessary. Her appearance would be shocking enough and she needed to make the most of it.

After changing her mind several times, she finally chose to wear the new Indian madras style in a shimmery turquoise shot with gold threads. The filmy dress with sleeves to the elbow, fell straight from the shoulders to the gold embroidered hem. Gold earrings and neutral leather sandals with a low wedge for walking comfort completed her outfit.

The last thing she wanted to do was embarrass Cord whose tall, rugged good looks turned female heads wherever he went. Possessing a physically powerful, hard-muscled physique with dark hair and eyes as dark as blue as cobalt, the attention he drew was a phenomenon Ashley had been forced to accept early in their relationship or jealousy would have torn her apart.

The only reason she could handle it was because he was oblivious to the stir that always surrounded him. The opposite of a vain man, he never thought of himself. Until Sheila, he'd never given Ashley any reason to think another woman filled his eyes or his thoughts.

Because from day one he'd made Ashley believe that she was his whole world, it was like a ghastly, sickening nightmare when she saw what was happening between him and his own stepmother.

Stop it, Ashley. The past no longer matters. You're here for Cord's welfare. Put everything else out of your mind or you'll go mad...

Taking several deep breaths to calm down, she approached the nursing station. ''Hello— Could you tell me where 521-C is?''

''Go down the first hall you see on your right and pass through the double doors. You can't miss it.''

Ashley muttered her thanks, picked up the suitcase and sewing bag which seemed to have grown heavier, and started off. As she rounded the corner, she saw a tall, dark-haired man coming through the doors halfway down the hall. Even from this distance he looked instantly familiar.

Cord.

All the air seemed to leave her trembling body. She could tell it was her husband by the way he carried himself, those long swift strides which were headed in her direction.

She hadn't had any sleep for the last two nights planning what she'd say to him when they first met again after all these months. But she didn't need to worry because he swept right past her, intent on reaching the main hall-way.

Had she changed so much?

Staggered that he didn't recognize her, she turned around to go after him, then froze in place because he suddenly swung on his heel and stared back at her in total disbelief.

They couldn't be more than six feet apart, yet it was close enough for her to watch the blood drain out of his face. He looked so gaunt, she thought he might faint. Because he was wearing the familiar pewter-gray business suit with the paisley silk tie she liked so much, she could tell he'd lost weight.

He looked ill.

''Hello, Cord.'' She managed to find her voice at last.

He drew closer, his intense gaze taking in her face and hair before inspecting every square inch of her pregnant body with eyes as frigid and dark as the Arctic. As each second ticked by, she saw the tightening of his chis-eled features, the way his body went rigid and his hands formed into fists at his sides.

A shadow passed over his face. ''Who's the father?'' he bit out with unconcealed fury.

CHAPTER TWO

ASHLEY shouldn't have been surprised by the question, but somehow she had expected any response, any comment, any question but that one. Her fidelity to him was not in question here! But incredibly it seemed that her husband believed someone else had fathered their child.

She supposed he could be forgiven for coming to that conclusion. But at the same time, did he honestly believe she could sleep with another man while she was still married to *him*?

What an amazing irony. She could have laughed out loud if she hadn't felt like sobbing.

"Can we talk about this in private?" she whispered because people were walking in the hallways from both directions. Right now his mood was too volatile to trust in the company of others.

Like an automaton, he picked up the bag and suitcase, then grasped her elbow in an almost painful grip. Before she knew how it had happened, he'd ushered them down another hallway to an open housekeeping storeroom.

"Cord—we can't come in here!" she cried softly.

"We just did."

He turned on a light and slammed the door, barring any hope of a quick exit with his unquestionably masculine frame.

She hadn't been this close to him for so long, she forgot how susceptible she was to his potent male appeal, the scent of the soap he used in the shower, the warmth of his hard body electrifying hers.

Strong hands reached out and covered her shoulders, forcing her closer, but her swollen belly prevented a merging of their bodies.

"Look at me," he demanded in a deceptively quiet voice.

Afraid to do otherwise, she lifted her head and met his piercing glance.

"Tell me who he is, Ashley." His voice grated.

She tried swallowing, but it was impossible. "I'm surprised you have to ask."

A glint of pain flashed in the depths of his eyes. "It's Greg's baby, isn't it?" came the tortured utterance.

"*Greg?*" she blurted incredulously.

The hands on her shoulders bit in to her skin. "He's always been crazy about you. It's the reason he hired you to work for him after we found out I couldn't give you a baby. It's the reason he's been so damn loyal to you. *Good Lord*— To think my wife and my best friend could get involved—" he ground out. His haunted tone devastated her.

Right now would be the perfect time to throw Sheila in his face and make him realize what their affair had done to her, Ashley. But she couldn't.

"Please, Cord. Your hands— You don't know your own strength." In his pain, he had unconsciously gripped her too hard.

When her entreaty got through to him, he let go of her, looking like the lone survivor of a horrendous battle.

Taking a deep draft of air she began to explain. "The night before I left the house, y-you came to my room, and you know what happened. Within a few weeks, I had all the signs of flu and went to see Dr. Noble.

"He ran a lot of tests, but everything came back normal. He joked with me that my symptoms sounded like morning sickness, then asked me when was the last time that you and I had slept together."

The whole time she was talking, Cord seemed to be looking straight through to her soul.

"One thing led to another and he decided to do a pregnancy test on me. He said stranger things had happened, that once in a while an infertile couple defied all the odds.

"When the first test came back saying I was pregnant, he did two more tests to be absolutely certain, then told me we'd made medical history."

Her proud chin lifted a little higher. "It's *your* baby, Cord. No one else's." Her voice throbbed.

A stillness came over him that pervaded the entire storeroom.

Like trick photography, his expression underwent a total transformation. Frame by frame she watched as if new life had just been breathed into his body. His well-defined chest heaved from the force of a dozen new emotions exploding inside him, needing expression.

Ashley could feel them because her body was undergoing a similar reaction. She'd lived with this secret knowledge too long, holding back for the moment when they were divorced and she was ready to tell him.

But circumstances had dictated that she tell him sooner, and now her husband knew the truth. With this knowledge, she realized everything was about to change...

''I presume you were going to tell me after the fact,'' came the acid comment.

A fresh wave of guilt swept over her. ''I— I thought it best to keep it to myself so our divorce would go through quickly. Sheila intimated that the two of you were anxious to—''

''Sheila be damned!'' he interrupted cruelly. ''You knew how much I've always wanted to have a baby, and you kept it from me. *Good Lord*, Ashley—''

Her heart almost failed her. ''But, Cord— Sheila said—''

"I don't ever want to hear her name mentioned again," he bit out with barely controlled rage. "When is our child due?"

"May thirtieth, four weeks from now."

"The day before *my* birthday," he murmured in wonder, as if to himself. "Have you had an ultrasound?" he asked unexpectedly.

"Yes. As far as the doctor can tell, the baby is perfect and it's a good size."

She saw a little nerve throb along his forceful jaw, evidence of the emotion he was experiencing.

"Are we having a boy or a girl?"

Ashley averted her eyes. "I don't know."

"Why not?" he fired back.

"I—I decided I wanted to be surprised, so I asked the doctor not to tell me. All I care about is that it's normal."

"It appears that if I hadn't called you, I wouldn't have known about our child until after it was born," he murmured, sounding far away. "What really made you come?"

It was hard to look anywhere except at him. "Greg said—" She paused, afraid to reveal too much. Talking about his best friend was like treading on sacred ground. She didn't know exactly what she should say.

"Tell me!"

She shook her head. "He was worried about you, that's all."

His eyes flickered dangerously. "He always did have a lot of influence over you."

It was on the tip of her tongue to remind him that Sheila had only to call him—ostensibly about a business problem—no matter what hour of the night, and he would leave Ashley in bed to take care of it.

But bringing up his stepmother's name at such a precarious moment as this could only exacerbate the tension between them.

To her shock, she felt his hand run through her hair, feeling the silky strands. She had to stifle a moan. "I like it," he whispered. "There's a lot of natural curl. I would imagine our baby will look just like you."

Don't touch me. Please don't touch me.

"Ashley—" he began, sounding more emotional than angry. But the door flew open and one of the ladies in housekeeping cried out to discover the two of them inside.

"Sorry." He grinned at the woman while escorting Ashley from the closet with a possessive arm around the back of her waist. "I had this irresistible urge to kiss my wife who's about to become a mother, and I didn't want an audience."

The woman tittered, obviously amused and charmed by him. "You can stay in there all day for all I care. Just let me put this waxer away."

Anyone else might have made the woman suspicious enough to call security, but Cord had a way with people that was fascinating to watch.

He brushed Ashley's flushed cheek with the back of his hand, sending a shiver of forgotten delight through her body. Eyeing her face through narrowed eyes he said, "I think maybe it was time we came out for air."

The custodian chuckled and waved them on, then went about her work. Ashley, still dizzy from the sensations his touch had aroused, walked unsteadily at his side, her wedges making a clicking sound on the linoleum as he opened the door for her so they could enter the floor where he'd been admitted.

As they neared the nursing station, a six-tyish-looking man in a lab coat looked up, then smiled at Cord. "It looks like you found your wife."

"I did. Ashley, this is Dr. Drake, the head of the clinic."

She said something appropriate and shook the doctor's hand, but the word "clinic" sent a shudder through her body. "W-what kind of clinic are you referring to?" she stammered. *Cancer? Or something equally serious?*

The doctor frowned in puzzlement. "Our couples program."

Couples?

"She just got here so we haven't had a chance to discuss anything yet," Cord explained, but Ashley could scarcely concentrate because she was still reacting to the doctor's comment.

She shook her head in bewilderment. "What program?"

Dr. Drake's attention switched to Cord. "I thought you explained things to her when you were in here on Friday."

Ashley swallowed hard. "I—I'm afraid I didn't give him an opportunity. We're getting a divorce and there's been virtually no contact.''

''Yes. Your husband confided as much to me. Mrs. McKnight? Can I assume you're here because you want to help your husband?''

After a moment's pause she murmured, ''Yes.''

''All right then. As you're aware, every year in our country we declare a day of no smoking.''

Smoking?

She couldn't imagine what he was getting at.

''Those trying to quit the habit abstain from cigarettes for twenty-four hours. In conjunction with that effort, we piloted a special program at City Creek ten years ago called the Great Salt Lake Smokeout.''

Ashley had heard of it.

''It was so successful, we've done it every year since. Six couples, where one or both have a smoking problem, voluntarily sign up on a first-come, first-serve basis, and stay together in a special clinic for a week free of charge. We provide intensive counseling and therapy to help them break the habit.''

Her mind was spinning. "Dr. Drake? Neither of us smokes!"

"Your husband had the habit in college, but he got off it when he went to work as a park ranger."

Ashley was dumbfounded. Cord had never told her that...

"Since your separation, he's taken it up again and wants desperately to quit, thus the reason he came to us. His case is one of several kinds we're looking for because he wasn't a smoker all his life.

"We believe this latest addiction is an outward sign of emotional stress and deep-seated problems possibly relating as far back as childhood. Problems he hasn't yet come to terms with.

"We've learned it's easier if the partner in the marriage goes through the counseling, as well, in order to help their spouse and/or themselves. Through a team effort, the prognosis for quitting altogether is excellent because many problems and side issues are aired with positive results.

"In your particular situation, facing a traumatic divorce has obviously triggered his need to begin smoking again, so you're the one he would require to be on hand to help him learn more about himself and dig deep for answers.

"You certainly don't have to agree to this. It would take an exceptionally strong person to revisit the scene of the crime so to speak and place yourself in a vulnerable position once more."

Ashley moaned because his comments pierced the very core of her turmoil.

"In fact in ten years, I only know of one other couple on the verge of divorce who entered together, and they left the program early. For them, it didn't work. But Mr. McKnight seems anxious to try.

"Today is our kickoff. I'm giving a lecture in the auditorium in five minutes. If you're interested in helping your husband, talk to him and let me know what you decide by the end of the hour. If you decide not to go through with the program, I'll need to give your place to the next couple on the list."

While her thoughts reeled, he patted Cord's shoulder, then walked down the corridor.

Stunned by the news that Cord was a smoker, she stood there in a daze. "When I married you, I thought I knew everything about you, but it's evident I only scratched the surface. All weekend I assumed that you must be dying of a terminal illness and Greg was afraid to tell me.

"Instead—I discover you're here because of a *smoking* problem! It's too absurd." An angry laugh escaped.

"It's serious to me," Cord said in a quiet voice. "Even more so now that I've found out you're pregnant."

Ashley didn't have a comeback for that. During the last six months of their broken marriage she had no idea what he did apart from her because they spent so little time together. He and Sheila, along with several subordinates, ran the administrative end of the lucrative McKnight potato chip company. The various plants located in northern Utah and Idaho had produced a phenomenal business for three generations and it was still growing to meet the demand.

Sheila smoked a lot. Ashley could always tell when Cord had been with her because he came home from the office with telltale signs of tobacco clinging to his clothes. Under those circumstances it would be easy enough for Cord to fall back into an old habit.

Naturally she wanted him to stop, if only for his own health's sake. She supposed that knowing he was about to become a father would provide the extra incentive.

But one week without Sheila? Ashley mused waspishly. She couldn't imagine how either Cord or his stepmother would survive that long without each other.

Yet he obviously felt he needed help or he wouldn't have checked in to the hospital. But a couples program?

She'd heard smoking was a very difficult habit to break, and she admired anyone who was successful. Certainly a program like the one run at the hospital sounded as if it might work because it was attempting to deal with a person's whole psyche.

She moistened her dry lips. ''It would never have occurred to me that you were a smoker.''

''I put it behind me when I went to work for the forest service and thought I'd licked it.'' There was a distant pause. ''Evidently I haven't. Now that you know the truth, I wouldn't blame you if you walked away.''

She took a shaky breath. "If I do that, then you won't be able to participate."

"It doesn't matter, Ashley. I can afford to get the help I need through individual therapy. But when I heard about the clinic, the idea of couples working on the problem together made a lot of sense."

She hated to admit that she agreed, but she had serious reservations. "I don't feel comfortable about taking the place of another couple who wouldn't otherwise have the funds to get this kind of help."

Cord's jaw tautened. "That was one of my concerns, too. I've already told Dr. Drake that if you did join me, I would insist on paying for our stay and the therapy involved.

His admission didn't surprise her. In all areas but one, Cord was the most honest, decent human being she'd ever known.

"It was a mistake to have called you," he muttered darkly. "If you're ready, I'll walk you out to your car."

He cupped her elbow to usher her toward the elevator, but she pulled back. His dark brows furrowed in question.

"Cord—since you've gone to this much trouble, I have to assume you're intent on quitting smoking. I'll stay through your first meeting with the therapist, but beyond that, I can't promise anything."

His body stilled. "You don't have to do that."

"I—I came this morning, Cord, and I'll see it through that far at least."

"But your job?"

"The person who was going to replace me when I went into labor is with Mrs. Bromwell now. Early this morning I made the decision that no matter what happened between you and me, I wouldn't be going back there. It's not going to be a problem since we all agreed that anything could have happened during these last four weeks."

"You're right. Our baby might decide to come early."

"It's possible," she admitted, "but the doctor says there's no sign of that yet."

"Frankly, I'm glad you're quitting work."

Ashley looked away, nervous and apprehensive over what she'd done, but she'd made a commitment and couldn't back out on it. "Excuse me while I make that call."

She turned to the desk clerk who allowed Ashley the use of the phone. All the time she talked to Mrs. Bromwell's daughter, she felt Cord's presence and it prevented her from concentrating. After promising to keep in touch with the family, Ashley hung up the receiver. "Shall we go to the auditorium?"

His gaze swept over her, concerned and reminiscently possessive. "Are you all right? Do you need anything first?"

"No, thank you. I'm fine."

"If you should feel any discomfort, I want to know about it." The one thing she knew about Cord was that he would take perfect care of her.

"I promise," she said in an effort to reassure him.

When they went inside, Dr. Drake was speaking at the podium, using an overhead projector to put some points across. Cord shifted his arm to her shoulders and guided her down the aisle to a vacant row where they took the first two seats. He placed her suitcase and bag in the aisle next to his.

Another surprise awaited her when he reached for her left hand. She could feel him brailling her rings, no doubt to ascertain that they were still there.

When she attempted to put her arm back in her lap, he exerted the slightest pressure which served as a warning not to try to free herself.

She had been afraid of this happening. Now that he knew he was about to become a father, he was feeling proprietorial of her. He might not be in love with her any longer, but he would love their child. She had no doubts about that. Because she was going to be the mother, he would do everything in his power to help and protect her.

Once they were alone again, she'd remind him that they were getting a divorce. He couldn't go on touching her, holding her whenever he felt like it.

Somehow she had to make him see that the only reason she was here was to provide an additional impetus to help him conquer the problem which had beset him.

"...After this general meeting, which should only take another ten minutes, we'll assign each couple a room and ask you to go there and get settled. Breakfast will be served at seven-thirty in the conference room next door.

"At eight o'clock, a psychologist will visit each couple in their rooms to begin the treatment and therapy sessions.

"Lunch will be at twelve, followed by a getting-acquainted session for everyone back in here at twelve-thirty.

"I believe that's as much as I need announce at this time. Right now, I'd like to introduce Mack and Barbara, a couple who were involved in our pilot program ten years ago.

"Mack was a heavy smoker who'd tried dozens of times to quit without success.

"Mack? Tell us what happened when you came in here."

Ashley tried to listen while the man explained how City Creek's program had turned his life around and made a new man of him. But with Cord sitting next to her, his lower thigh brushing against her nylon-clad leg, she couldn't possibly concentrate.

While he held her hand, he absently rubbed his thumb over her palm. Every motion sent her pulse skyrocketing, rekindling old desires which had been lying dormant over the last eight months.

She could hardly breathe as she felt his gaze wander over the pregnant line of her body. He was studying her, most likely comparing what he saw to his last memory of her. It shamed her now to remember how she'd molded herself to him after a rapturous night of lovemaking. But the second she'd fallen asleep, he'd stolen from the bedroom she was using, and had gone back to his own room.

When she'd awakened and had discovered him missing, she went to find him, needing to talk about what had happened.

During the night he'd begged her to believe him, that there had been no affair with Sheila. After what they'd just shared, she'd wanted to have faith in him and thought maybe this could be a new beginning.

But the conversation she had in mind never took place because when she reached the door of his room, she heard Sheila's voice. She was talking to Cord.

Though Ashley felt like she was going to faint from the pain, she peered inside. What she saw turned out to be the blackest moment of her life.

Within ten minutes she'd packed a suitcase and had left the house in the compact car he'd bought her. Since that hellish morning, she hadn't stepped over the threshold of the McKnight house. She never would again.

"Ashley? It's time to go to our room. The others have already filed out."

Cord's low voice brought her back to the present with a jolt. Her head jerked around. "What?"

His lancing eyes searched her features relentlessly. He let out an expletive. "You've gone pale."

"I'm just feeling a little empty inside," she lied. "It's nothing serious.'

"What can I get you? Some juice? I saw a machine in the hall."

"That sounds good."

"Let's go."

After having been on her own for over half a year, she had to admit it felt wonderful to be taken care of again. No one was more solicitous of her needs than Cord. He'd been a giver from the first moment she'd met him. That quality in him hadn't changed.

Within a couple of minutes he'd whisked her to their room a few doors down the hall and had forced her to sit down at the side of the bed, guarding her to make sure she drank every drop of the canned orange juice.

Though she hadn't needed a drink, it tasted delicious. While she emptied the can, he put the bag in the closet, then lifted her suitcase onto his bed and started emptying it.

Ridiculous as it seemed, though she'd been married to him for six years, she felt shy and a little embarrassed as he unpacked her things, particularly her nightgowns and underwear.

''What are these?'' He held several vials of pills in his hand.

''Prenatal vitamins and calcium tablets.''

He put them on the top of the dresser. ''How often do you take them?''

''The vitamins once a day. The calcium, twice.''

Any normal man who'd just found out he was going to be a father would show some curiosity. But this was Cord who'd been told by specialists that he would probably never be able to father a child.

Yet the miracle had happened. He was about to become a new dad. She could see the excitement in his eyes every time they rested on her. More, she could feel it in the huskiness of his deep voice. He couldn't seem to keep his hands off her.

This was *his* baby she was carrying. His natural curiosity had been magnified a dozen times by the wondrous news. Ashley had to resign herself to the fact that he'd already taken over his role as prospective father with a seriousness that bordered on overprotectiveness.

In her heart she couldn't blame him. Right now she didn't think that even Sheila could wield enough power to win him away from Ashley's side, no matter the urgency. Once she'd delivered, it would be a different story. In the meantime, it was evident Cord would be preoccupied with thoughts of the son or daughter almost ready to be born.

If Sheila already hated Ashley now, how much more would that emotion escalate when she found out Ashley was carrying Cord's baby?

Instead of his stepmother somehow finding out *first* and running to Cord with the information—no doubt twisting it in some strange way to make Ashley look bad in his eyes, Ashley derived a certain satisfaction in knowing that Cord would have to inform Sheila he was about to be a new father. That would definitely come as a shock!

She bit her lip. How long would Cord wait before he excused himself to use the clinic phone and make that important call?

Following the thought, she wondered how much the baby would put a crimp in his future plans with Sheila, whatever they were.

If Cord married her, that would mean she'd be the other woman in their child's life. Ashley couldn't fathom such an untenable possibility.

"Come on, Ashley. You're still looking wan. Let's get you to the dining room for some solid food."

"I'm really not hungry, but I'm sure you are. Why don't you go without me? I ate something before I came and the juice filled me up.

Besides, my back is aching a little, and I would like to lie down till the psychologist arrives.''

He pondered her remarks with a single-minded intensity reminiscent of the old Cord she'd first met and fallen in love with. ''Then let me help you relax.''

Faster than she could think to lift her legs from the floor, he leaned down and gathered her in his arms to help her stretch out properly on top of the bed.

His gentle solicitation, the close proximity of their bodies produced a bittersweet ache. She turned her head toward the wall, afraid to look at him. ''It's a little cool in here for you, I think.'' In the next instant he'd found a light blanket to cover her.

''Th-thank you,'' she whispered. The words came out haltingly because as he tucked it around her, his hands seemed to have a mind of their own. She squeezed her eyelids tightly together as she felt him shape his palms to the large mound containing their baby and begin a slow exploration.

You don't have the right, Cord! Not when you've been intimate with Sheila, her heart sobbed in silence.

But Ashley felt powerless to stop him.

Because you're still in love with him and crave any contact with him. Admit it!

His sure touch was light as a feather, but she felt it in every atom of her trembling body. It had been eight months since she'd known such exquisite pleasure. Eight lonely, interminably long, desolate months. She never wanted him to stop.

"It's a miracle, darling—" she heard him murmur in a thick-toned voice.

Suddenly the blanket disappeared and the weight on her stomach felt a little heavier. She opened her eyes and turned her head back around to discover his face buried against her belly. A slight gasp escaped her throat as he started to kiss her through the filmy material of her dress.

Unshed tears sprang to her eyes. From almost the very first moment they'd met, he'd kissed her under every conceivable circumstance and manner, but she'd never been as moved, never felt as worshiped and adored as she did at this moment.

Cord would never have the experience of carrying a child nine months inside his own body. Yet it was *his* child. She realized this was the closest he could come to sharing the experience with her. But she hadn't counted on the indescribable swell of emotion that made her want to forget every painful thing that had gone on in the past and just feast on this incredible feeling of oneness with him.

A little being was growing inside her, getting bigger every day. A little life which was half her, half Cord. But while she'd had over eight months to ponder the wonder of it all, he'd only just learned that his life was already immortalized by the son or daughter waiting to make an appearance shortly.

Being pregnant with Cord's baby bonded them in a way that went far beyond the physical world and touched on the eternal. She couldn't begrudge him the God-given right to fatherhood by denying him this miraculous moment of discovery.

It was something she would treasure in her heart, long after they'd separated and gone their own way. *Which they would*, a nagging inner voice cried out in despair once more.

"I'll be right back," he whispered, pressing a hard, swift kiss to her astonished mouth. After covering her again with the blanket, he left the room in a few swift strides.

CHAPTER THREE

"HELLO, you two. I'm Vincent Warren, but since we're going to be getting to know each other very, very well—" He grinned. "Why don't you just call me Vince."

"That sounds good to us," Cord spoke for both of them in a deep, even voice. He sat down in a chair next to her bed, drinking a cup of coffee he'd carried from the dining room. Out of thoughtfulness, he'd brought her back a roll and some grapefruit, in case she got hungry later.

Seated on the edge of the bed, Ashley tried to put the memory of those moments before Cord had gone for breakfast out of her mind. It had been a transcendent experience, one which had shaken her and affected her ability to concentrate.

She did note that the middle-aged psychologist emanated a professional mien in his pale blue lab coat and clipboard. He was clean-shaven, unlike so many in his profession.

"Ashley? Is that what you want me to call you?"

She nodded.

"And you, sir? You wish to be called Cord?"

"All right." He put everything on the bedside table, then reached in his pocket. "I'm going to adhere this patch to your neck, Cord. As you know, this is one of the methods used to help you lose your desire for a cigarette."

"Are there any side effects associated with it?" Ashley blurted anxiously, causing Cord to flash her a questioning glance.

She turned to Vince. "H-he had a bad reaction once to some pain medication following a brush with a grizzly bear."

"That's right," Cord muttered. "I'd forgotten."

"Oh, honestly, Cord. How could you possibly forget an experience that almost cost you your life?" she cried out in remembered pain.

"Really!" Vince made a notation on his legal pad. "That's a story I'd like to hear about later. What was prescribed?"

"Percodan," she supplied instantly.

"Then you're probably allergic to codeine. The patch doesn't have the same ingredients, so I'm not worried, but we'll watch you carefully all the same. Most people respond favorably to this form of treatment. We'll just have to wait and see."

It took him about one minute for the procedure, then Vince reached for a chair and sat down facing them.

"I'm sure Dr. Drake has already explained this, but the aim of our clinic is to put together a profile on both of you so we can get as indepth a picture of your life as possible. At the same time, we'll teach you some strategies to end your compulsion to smoke.

"As you know, human nature is such that we all operate under the selective memory process. Interviewing both of you at the same time helps get two points of view on the same happening, and supplies the missing pieces to help us make the most correct assessment possible.

"What happened just now when your wife remembered an incident in your life that you didn't deem very important, is a case in point.

"I've read the summary of your work profile and understand you lived a lot of your life in the out-of-doors before moving back to Salt Lake. Obviously the accident such as she described was routine to you, but to your wife, it constituted much more of a threat, thus her reaction and instant recall.

"You see how beneficial interviewing both of you simultaneously will work to our advantage?"

Ashley was very much afraid that she did. When she darted a covert glance at Cord, his closed expression told her nothing about his inner thoughts.

"Willpower and self-mastery are always the keys to living a temperate life," Vince expounded, "but many other factors get in the way. When two people live together, for good or bad, those factors increase, thus the reason for both of you agreeing to go through the program. By the end of the week, we hope to have accomplished a great deal.

"Cord—we'd like to see you walk out of here feeling physically fit and having less of an urge to light up because number one, it's unhealthy. Number two, because through counseling here, you will have zeroed in on the stumbling blocks in your life that trigger your need for nicotine, and will have taken positive steps to remove them.''

Ashley stirred restlessly on the bed. Once they got into the past, it would be like opening Pandora's box. She dreaded what was about to come out and wondered if she had the temerity to last the course.

Vince's gaze centered on her. "If you get uncomfortable sitting there while I'm interviewing, please move around or lie down, or do whatever makes you the most comfortable."

"Thanks. I'm fine for the moment." Physically, she'd had a very easy pregnancy. Except for occasional back pain, she didn't swell that much and the morning sickness left after the third month. *It's my emotional state that is in turmoil. Being with Cord like this is killing me.*

The psychologist nodded. "According to the notes Dr. Drake left with me, I see that you were the one who filed for divorce. Is that correct?"

"Yes."

"How long have you been separated?"

"Eight months."

''When was the last time you saw each other since the separation?''

She bowed her head to avoid Cord's searching gaze. ''This morning.''

''So there's been no communication until now?''

''Not until last Friday when Cord phoned me.''

''Yet you cared enough to help him, and he cared enough to ask for your help. That's a good beginning if we're to accomplish anything positive in the next seven days.'' He cleared his throat. ''All right. Cord? Let's start with you. What's your age?''

''Thirty-six.''

''From what I understand, you didn't start smoking until you went away to college.''

''That's right,'' he answered quietly. Ashley kept her eyes on Vince, but she was listening to Cord with every part of her being.

''Had you ever been tempted by cigarettes before that time?''

''No.''

''Most kids start in junior high or high school. What do you think made you take the first one so late in life?''

''I don't know. I was at a loose end, and the fellows who roomed in the same apartment I did all smoked. One night at a party someone offered me a cigarette and I thought, 'why not?' That's how it started.''

''We'll assume for the moment that you've been at a loose end many times long before then and since. So what was different about that time?''

Ashley heard the draft of air Cord took in before he answered.

''I'd just left home after a bitter scene with my father.''

''Your mother didn't figure in it?''

''No.''

One of Ashley's deepest disappointments was not ever meeting or knowing Cord's mother, a woman he'd adored. As for Cord's father, he was a cold man, aloof.

''You were what? Eighteen?'' Cord nodded. ''Tell me more about your family. How many brothers and/or sisters?''

''I'm an only child.''

Vince wrote more notations. ''Since you went away to school in the East, am I assuming correctly that you generally made several visits home a year?''

''No,'' came the abrupt reply.

This was news to Ashley. Her gaze fastened compulsively on him, her heart thudding.

''Why not?''

At this point Cord leaned forward, his hands clasped between his knees in an attitude of solemnity. ''My father and I became estranged before I graduated from high school.''

''Why?''

Cord's face darkened with lines. ''From the time I was fourteen, I always had to work for my father at the office doing odd jobs, anything he wanted me to do. It was always intended that I would head the family business after he retired, so he expected me to know it all.'' His voice grated.

''I take it the idea of filling his shoes didn't appeal to you.''

''No. I had interests which ran in another direction entirely, but being the only son, I felt trapped.''

''You never told me that—'' Ashley blurted.

Cord absently brushed his lower lip with his thumb. "I never said anything because my mother urged me to do what my father wanted. Above all, I hated disappointing her."

"Surely she wanted your welfare above all else!"

Sadness lurked in Cord's eyes. "I'm positive of it. But because Dad didn't seem capable of making her happy, I thought I could. Anyway, in May of my senior year, about three weeks before graduation, Dad hired a new girl to replace the receptionist who was leaving to get married."

Suddenly Cord's dark glance swerved to Ashley. "Her name was Sheila Wright."

A gasp came out of Ashley. "You really did know her clear back then?" she cried in fresh agony. "Then that means Sheila was telling the truth." For the second time in one morning, she watched Cord's face pale.

Vince got to his feet before she did. "All right. The mention of this Sheila has touched on an issue of extreme sensitivity, one that has obviously not been resolved." He eyed Ashley compassionately. "Is Sheila the person you feel is partially responsible for the breakup of your marriage?''

''Among other reasons.'' Ashley's voice shook. She felt ill. ''I've got to get out of here.''

''*Ashley*—''

She heard the tormented plea in Cord's tone, but she couldn't handle the gut-wrenching revelation that Sheila had been his lover as far in the past as high school! Sheila had intimated that she'd been the other woman in the background of Cord's life, but Cord had always denied it.

Somehow Ashley had thought *she* was the only person important to Cord before they were married...

''If you'll excuse us, Cord, I'd like to speak to Ashley in private.''

She had barely made it out the door when Vince caught up with her. ''I can see you're in pain, Ashley. The more we delve, the more it's going to hurt. But I want you to think about a couple of things before you leave the hospital.

''Without your help, your husband can't remain here on this particular program. It takes two.''

She knew that, but she feared that if she heard any more, it would destroy her.

''We haven't been going ten minutes, yet already you've learned several new things about your husband's past. Wouldn't you rather know the whole truth, instead of just bits and pieces, before you walk away from your marriage?

''Dr. Drake said you didn't know your husband had ever had a smoking problem. It's obvious your husband is a very private person. Apparently he has a history of keeping certain memories to himself which are destructive to him and hurting you now. If you were to stay the entire week, perhaps we'll find out why he has chosen to remain silent on so many issues.

''In the end, you will have greater understanding of his psyche. So will he. Unburdening himself could be the key to getting over his habit. If you do go through with the divorce, the time spent here will give you closure on your marriage.

"After what I've just witnessed, I can promise you that your divorce *will not* resolve the pain and doubts still assailing you. For your mental health *and* his, I urge you to see this through.

"If you can't, then I suggest you make an appointment to talk to Dr. Drake. He's one of the finest psychiatrists in the country. You need some help before your baby comes. The emotional burdens you're carrying will affect your child. Think about it."

Ashley rubbed her forehead where she could feel the beginnings of a headache. "I know you're right, Vince. It's just so hard."

"Because you're still in love with him."

She would have liked to deny it, but because he'd spoken the truth, she couldn't.

"No matter how difficult this is, think what it will mean to your child's happiness if you and Cord can deal with this now. Whether you stay married, or end up divorced, you'll both be able to start fresh, with new faith in the future. Hopefully he'll be able to live the rest of his life without a crutch like nicotine."

Vince spoke the truth. There was more at stake here than just her pain and Cord's. Their baby deserved the best from both of them. She'd told Cord she would only stay as long as the first session took but the therapist's words found a responding chord in her and prevented her from leaving.

Somehow she was going to have to find the strength to sit there and listen to more devastating details of his long-term affair with Sheila.

"I'm sorry I walked out," she said quietly.

"It was a normal reaction, Ashley."

"If I'm going to stay on, I guess I'm going to have to find another way to deal with my pain."

"If you'll keep your thoughts focused on what's best for your child in the long run, I think you'll be able to handle it." After a pause, "Do you want to wait until after the group session this afternoon to pick up where we left off?"

She shook her head. "No—the sooner everything is out in the open, the better."

"Good for you."

As she turned, she saw Cord standing in the doorway to their room, his features an expressionless mask. "This is asking too much of you, Ashley. You said you'd stay through the first session. I won't hold you to any more.''

She took a fortifying breath. ''I admit I'd rather be anywhere than here.'' At that comment, she thought she saw a flicker of pain enter his eyes before they darkened. ''But Vince is right. If you never tell me the whole truth, and I never stay long enough to listen, then we'll carry around unwanted baggage the rest of our lives. That won't be good for the baby. So, for the sake of our unborn child, I'll stay.''

Her words brought another grimace to his hardened features. ''I can't ask for more than that.'' He studied her so thoroughly, she started feeling weak-kneed again. ''Are you sure you're up to this physically?''

''I'll be fine.''

She moved past him, but her protruding stomach brushed against his arm. The slightest contact sent a current of electricity through her body. To offset the sensation, she sat down on the bed next to the bedside table and began eating the roll and grapefruit he'd brought in earlier. Maybe a little sustenance would help insulate her against the shocks still to come.

When Vince started the questioning again, Cord stood nearby, his hands on the back of one of the metal chairs. The knuckles stood out white, testimony of the tension gripping him.

"You said that you and your father became estranged, then you mentioned the woman, Sheila. Let's start there."

The last of the roll turned to sawdust in Ashley's mouth as she listened without looking in his direction.

"Sheila was twenty-five when Dad hired her, seven years older than I. She was a willowy blonde who knew she was attractive. I noticed that she flirted with all the male employees, married or single, even my father."

"Did she flirt with you?"

"Especially with me."

Ashley's eyes closed tightly.

"I was like a lot of high school guys, flattered by the attention of an older woman. Since I already had a legitimate right to be at work until late, I hung around there a lot more, hoping she'd hang around, too.

"One night I got my wish. She didn't have her car and needed a ride home. So I willingly drove her to her apartment. She invited me to come up for a drink.

"I couldn't believe my luck, so I went inside her place. After she put on some music and told me to get comfortable on the couch, she brought out a couple of beers.

"Since I'd thought she meant a Coke or something, I was really excited because she was treating me like a man her own age which really built my ego. I drank beer with her. Then she asked me if I wanted to dance. Another thrill.

"Before I knew it, we were kissing."

Ashley could hardly breathe.

"She'd obviously been around and knew what she was doing. Though I'd had my share of girlfriends, I'm afraid I wasn't as experienced. After about a half hour, she wanted to move things to the bedroom.

"I'd never slept with a woman before. It suddenly dawned on me that my first time ought to be with a girl my own age, someone I really cared about—not one of dad's employees who might spread tales and get me in trouble.

"Sheila represented forbidden fruit, a conquest if you like, but my hormones rather than my emotions were involved. I remember feeling very foolish and regretting like hell that I'd gone up to her apartment.

"She laughed at me when I told her I had to get home or my parents would be upset. Her taunts were another wound to my pride, but I got out of there before I made the ultimate mistake. *Thank God.*"

The violence of his emotions reduced Ashley to a trembling lump of flesh. She had a dozen new questions. *You sound like you're telling the truth, Cord. Are you?*

"When I got home," he continued, "my father was waiting up for me. He was livid. Apparently he'd called the office and the night custodian told him I'd left the office with Sheila some time ago.

"Without filling in between the lines, I told Dad that I had given her a lift home because she didn't have her car. He obviously knew much more than that had happened. He could probably smell the beer. In any event, he was angrier than I'd ever seen him in my life. He slapped my face."

Ashley stared at him in horror. ''Your father actually hit you for that?''

''Yes. Unfortunately Mother had heard us arguing and she came in the living room in time to witness it. On that particularly black night I grew up, putting my adolescence and innocence behind me.

''Dad never apologized. He ordered me to stay away from the office and told me that I'd be spending the summer in Idaho, working at one of the potato chip plants.

''For the last remaining weeks the three of us avoided each other around the house, never referring to the incident again. I was glad to be going away for the summer because it meant I didn't have to be in his company.

''When fall approached, I came home to tell my mother I wanted to stay in Utah and get a degree in forestry and land management. But she begged me to go on to Cornell and study finance and business. Dad had been planning that for me since my childhood.

''Mother was afraid of him, but I never realized how serious the problem was until that time. It was then I began to see that if I didn't go, he might take it out on Mother since he counted on her influence to persuade me. So I went away to school. But the truth of the matter was, Cornell had always been *his* dream, not mine.''

The bitterness of his tone infiltrated every particle of Ashley's being. She was devastated by what she'd just heard.

Cord relinquished the chair and put a hand in his pocket. His solid, well-honed body paced the floor for a silent interval.

''As I told you earlier, it was during my first year away at college that I picked up the habit of smoking. Near the end of the second semester, Mother wrote that she was going in for a hysterectomy. But what should have been routine surgery became something else. She had complications and contracted pneumonia. I flew home to spend the last few days in the hospital with her before she died.''

The pain in his voice haunted Ashley.

''Dad and I were speaking again, but there was a distance between us that could never be breached.

''After the funeral I flew back to Cornell and resumed my studies, but by the middle of my sophomore year, I couldn't lie to myself any longer. I didn't want to be there and had no intentions of going into the family business. Throughout that period I was smoking pretty heavily.

"Finally, I withdrew from school and flew home for the Christmas holidays with the intention of enrolling at Utah State in Logan, Utah. It was night when the taxi dropped me off in front of the house. I had no way of knowing if Dad was home because I hadn't checked the garage.

"I called to him—there was no answer. When I took my bags upstairs, I thought I heard laughter coming from his bedroom. So I rapped on his door and peeked inside."

Ashley knew what was coming and sat there in terrified silence.

"Another woman was in the bed he'd shared with my mother. It was Sheila."

A moan escaped while she tried to stifle the pain she imagined he must have felt for so many reasons.

"When it didn't work with the son, I suppose she decided to try it on the father, who was in his late fifties and old enough to be her father. I didn't stick around for explanations.

Instead, I took off in my car and drove to Logan where I worked any number of odd jobs to pay for my tuition and board.

"Through a friend, Dad found out where I was living and came to see me. At best, it was a pathetic meeting. He said he grieved for Mother, but the house was empty without her and he'd fallen in love with Sheila who was now his private secretary and fast becoming his right hand in the business.

"He explained that they suited each other and were planning to get married quietly at home. He wanted me to be there. I said no and asked him to leave.

"After that, I buried myself in schoolwork. A lot of my credits transferred from Cornell and I was able to finish up in four years time with a degree in forestry.

"As a graduating senior, several government agencies interviewed me for jobs at different areas around the country, but the one I wanted was the ranger job in Teton National Park.

"I decided to check it out first and met a guy, Art Williams, who was the chief ranger. From the start we seemed to hit it off. There were many things to admire about him, but above all he was physically fit for the work which involved a lot of mountaineering.

"I couldn't go far without being winded. He sized me up fast. He said that a guy who was born to live in the back country, yet still had trouble catching his breath, had to be a smoker. When I said yes, he told me there were fifty other guys applying for the job, but it was mine if I'd quit. I guess I wanted it badly enough that I stopped."

Ashley saw Vince cock his head and stare at Cord. "Was it difficult?"

"No. Not really. Every day of abstention I felt better. There was too much work to do, and I enjoyed the job more than anything I'd ever done in my life."

"Now that you look back on it, Cord, can you see that there might have been an underlying reason why you no longer needed the nicotine?"

Cord looked pensive. "Yes. I was no longer feeling any pressure from home and could please myself."

"Exactly." Vince rose from the chair. "Think about that during lunch. After the group session, we'll talk some more. Right now I'm going to leave you two alone and I'll see you here at two o'clock.''

Ashley dreaded his leaving, but she couldn't very well call him back to provide a needed buffer.

To her surprise, Cord headed for the door. ''I'm going outside for a short walk before lunch. Is there anything I can get for you before I go?''

Her emotions were in chaos. On the one hand, she feared being alone with him because they'd touched on so much that was new and painful. Conversely, it angered her that he would just walk out, leaving her to internalize all this information without further explanation.

Every revelation had brought new questions. She hardly knew where to start.

''According to the rules Dr. Drake presented, we're supposed to be together at all times, like a buddy system.''

His dark blue eyes glittered dangerously. ''We're hardly buddies, Ashley. I get the distinct feeling you'd like to be as far away from me as possible. Since you're pregnant and need to rest, I'll be the one to do the honors. Don't worry. I'm not about to light up yet.''

"Please, Cord. I didn't mean to intimate that you couldn't be trusted. Don't go— W-we need to talk.''

His mouthed tightened to a pencil-thin line. ''That's all I've been doing this morning.''

She took a deep breath. ''That wasn't talking. You were giving Vince facts. There's a world of difference.''

His gaze seemed to impale her. ''But you still consider it fiction.''

''I didn't say that!'' she defended hotly.

He folded his arms in an intimidating gesture. ''Which part did you believe?''

Ashley avoided his gaze and sat down on the chair Vince had just vacated. She needed some support at her back. ''Why didn't you ever tell me about Sheila? About what happened when you were eighteen?''

''The truth?'' he muttered thickly.

''That's why I'm here,'' came her tremulous response.

After a long pause, ''Because I knew from the time you first met her that she intimidated you. I didn't want to tell you anything that could feed your insecurity and contribute to your fears.''

She fought tears. ''But don't you see? By withholding that information from me, it made everything so much worse. Whenever she baited me, she insinuated that you two had a history, one you emphatically denied until today!''

''That's because we didn't have a relationship or anything remotely close to it. I didn't sleep with her.'' His voice grated. ''But with hindsight, I can see I made a grave mistake in not telling you what happened at the office that night. Do you believe me, Ashley?''

His question permeated the very air they were breathing.

''Yes. As far as your explanation goes,'' she added on a whisper.

She knew the last remark would enflame him, but she couldn't recall it because that wouldn't be staying true to herself.

He took a long time before he responded.

''If you could believe what I just told you in front of Vince, why can't you believe that there never was an affair, at any time?'' The words came out like a low-decibel hiss.

"Sheila is an accomplished liar who had an agenda from the moment Dad hired her for that secretarial job years ago.

"It's taken me a long time to admit that my parents' marriage was a disaster, a merger of two families with enough money to create a dynasty.

"Dad didn't love Mother. I wouldn't be surprised if he'd been unfaithful to her even before Sheila came along. Mother should have divorced him, but she didn't have the courage because in spite of everything, she was in love with him."

"That's tragic," she whispered.

Cord's features hardened. "Dad gave himself away when he slapped me. Obviously he wanted Sheila for himself and was furious she'd shown an interest in me."

They were wading into the very core of her pain. Ashley couldn't stay seated.

"You admit you were strongly attracted to her, too," she still felt compelled to remind him.

"Not strongly, Ash. I was a typical teen, with a crush on a blonde bombshell. Like most boys my age, I was going through an experimental stage. Don't tell me you didn't do the same, because I wouldn't believe you. But we're deviating from the real point. Any interest I had in Sheila died a certain death at her apartment when she assumed I would go to bed with her. That was never my intention.''

Ashley had no comeback for that. ''If that's true,'' she continued emotionally, ''then why did you quit your job with the forest service and expect us to move back in the house with her after your father died?''

When Cord didn't say anything for a minute, Ashley had the impression he was about to tell her something else she didn't know. *More secrets. It was a nightmare. All of it.*

CHAPTER FOUR

"IT WAS all part of a plan I conceived to get rid of Sheila, but it backfired and lost me my wife!"

Ashley reeled from the despair in his voice, but she couldn't refrain from asking him, "What plan?"

"The one I put into action after Mother's attorney, Ray Crawford, came to see me at the hospital the day Dad died. He informed me that half the house was in Mother's name, therefore half the house was legally mine."

"*What?*"

"That's right. Dad had drawn up his own will giving Sheila the house, but Mother's will superceded it. Dad didn't want me to have anything. It was his way of slapping me down again for attracting his girlfriend first, for not graduating from Cornell and spoiling all his plans for me.

''If you recall, when you and I visited Dad in the hospital following the plane crash, I had a word with him alone first.''

She nodded, remembering the uncomfortably long wait in the hospital lounge watching a dry-eyed Sheila pace, neither of them saying anything.

When Cord finally opened the door and beckoned them to come in, she felt his pain, but assumed it was because his father was seconds away from dying.

''I had the foolish hope that because he was so close to death, he and I could come to some kind of understanding about the past. But all he had to say to me was that Sheila would be his voice in the company now. He also intimated that since I had abandoned him to live in the Tetons, he was leaving the house to her.''

''He said *that*?'' she cried out once more. ''No words of love or comfort for you?'' She couldn't fathom it. ''Why didn't you tell me?''

The bleak expression in his eyes haunted her. ''I was too angry, Ashley. There'd been so much ugly history from the past, I didn't know how to deal with it, and I refused to burden you when we were already having problems in our marriage. Another mistake I bitterly regret.''

''But that's *horrible*!''

''He was a horrible man. Evidently he didn't think I would ever find out, but Mother's attorney knew her wishes and made sure that I knew them. Ray and I talked it over, and I came to the decision to fight her and my father, but I had to be careful how I proceeded.

''My first strategy after the funeral was to tell Sheila that you and I were moving back in the house so she wouldn't have to be alone in her grief. I knew she intimidated you, but at that point in time I had no way of knowing about all the private conversations you'd had with Sheila or how much damage she'd already done to you.''

Ashley moaned, assailed by her own guilt. ''That's true. I never told you the things she said, b-because I didn't want to believe them.''

''She was a past master at manipulation, but I decided to take her on. Through Mother, I still had a place on the board if I chose to be active.

''From the time of Mother's death to this day, the board members have wanted me back in the company. In fact, they kept begging me to give up my ranger job, but I couldn't do that. I was too happy with my work, with you.''

We were happy, Cord.

''But when Dad died, I knew how they'd feel when they heard that Sheila had taken over his role and had been given his shares of stock. That's when I decided that I had to give up my park job and come back to the family business.

''By that point, you and I weren't communicating as well, and I thought maybe you'd be happier in Salt Lake around your old friends. But I never intended it to be a permanent move. I despised Sheila.''

Ashley flung her head back. ''I saw how much you despised her, Cord.''

Her body tautened. ''I was playing a role, Ashley. I pretended to be civil to her and get along until the time came when the board members could legitimately oust her from the business altogether. Then I'd force her out of the house with some kind of payoff.''

His eyes narrowed. "Unfortunately, I underestimated her ability to hurt you. She was and is an opportunistic exploiter who deliberately undermined our marriage by driving you away. But mark my words, one day I'm going to beat her at her own game, and she'll be long gone from our lives."

Cord sounded deadly serious, but Ashley knew what she'd seen in Cord's bedroom. It had been no hallucination.

"She's also an amazingly beautiful woman, and was able to captivate both you and your father."

His body went rigid. "You honestly think I found her attractive once I found out she'd been sleeping with my father?" Cord didn't raise his voice. Rather he spoke in a deadly soft tone. It sent shivers down her spine.

"Sometimes you can't help what you feel."

"A fatal attraction?" he interjected with a sneer.

She hung her head. "Yes."

"Give me the dates and places my supposed liaisons occurred, Ashley. Better yet, ask me to take a lie detector test."

"I don't need any proof. I saw it with my own eyes."

"When?" he demanded, his whole expression primitive.

"Worried, Cord?"

He stared at her for an interminably long moment without saying anything. Eventually he shook his head. "No. But it's getting through to me that you *think* you saw something so damning in your eyes, you walked out on me hours after we'd made love."

Her heart was beating too hard. Her breathing had grown shallow. "Vince was right. Two people can recall the same event with diametrically opposed points of view."

"What are you saying?"

"Don't you remember?" she reminded him. "As soon as I fell asleep, you left my bed."

"That's true. If I'd stayed, I wouldn't have been able to control myself and I would have made love to you again. After what we'd shared, I had a lot of thinking to do about us and our future."

"You're a liar, Cord!" she cried out. "You went straight back to your own bed where Sheila was waiting."

"And you witnessed all this with your own eyes?"

"Yes."

"That means you were coming to find me." The satisfaction in those words twisted the knife a little more.

"Oh, I found you all right." By now her hands had curled into fists.

"Tell me exactly what you saw." While she shook convulsively, he stood calm as water in a still pond.

"Sheila was lying on your bed," she began, "in a very provocative pose. She had put on your kelly-green bathrobe, the one I gave you on our first wedding anniversary. The one you'd worn to my room.' Her voice quavered precariously. "The belt was undone, and she wasn't wearing anything underneath."

"Go on."

"She'd been in the shower because I could see the wet hair dangling from the towel she'd wrapped around her head."

"All right. Now tell me where *I* was," he muttered as an all-consuming rage seemed to have overpowered him.

"You were in the shower. I could hear it running. She was talking to you. She called out to you, 'Cord, darling. Come back to bed. I miss you.'" Ashley stood straighter. "Please don't insult me by attempting to deny it."

A dark brow lifted menacingly. "I wouldn't dream of it. Unlike you, I believe you saw what you saw. The problem is, I wasn't there, so I have no way of knowing what that liar did or didn't do. I have to rely on your testimony completely."

Ashley blinked. "But you *were*," she insisted, a little less sure of herself than before.

He put his hands on his hips in an unconscious masculine stance. "Did you see me? Did you hear me answer her?"

"Well, no, but—"

"For your information, I went back to the room, put on my clothes and went for a long walk. I returned when I thought you'd had enough sleep and I could waken you to tell you my plans for us. But you had gone. There was no sign of you."

Could he fake the wealth of loss in his voice just now?

Cord could be so convincing, she didn't know what to think. ''W-what plans?''

''To forsake the families who needed a champion to fight against Sheila, to allow her the complete takeover of an established business to which she gained the rights through immoral and corrupt devices, to let her keep the whole damn house and everything that went with it. In other words, to let her win.

''And all because I wanted you more than anything else in this life. Because I wanted to go back to the Tetons where we were happy and live out the rest of our lives.''

Ashley felt a jabbing pain in the region of her heart. It propelled her to the window where she could view the foliage surrounding the state capitol. Many of the flowering trees were in blossom. A sign of spring and hope.

Had Sheila, with her posturing and innuendos, truly been trying to break up their marriage during those hellish two months after Cord's father died?

Had her jealousy driven her over the edge when she found out that Ashley and Cord slept together that last night?

Did she really want Cord so badly, she would resort to something as wicked as pretending to be with Cord in his bedroom so Ashley would think the worst?

Ashley closed her eyes, but the answer stared her in the face. She'd taken one look in Cord's room, had seen what Sheila had intended for her to see and on cue had fled the scene, never looking back, never giving Cord a chance to explain.

When she really thought about what he'd just told her, Ashley had to admit that she hadn't seen Cord in that bedroom. She'd only seen evidence that he'd been in there. In all honesty, she never did hear his voice answering Sheila.

Was it possible Sheila had put on that act solely for Ashley's benefit?

''While you're attempting to sort through her sea of lies and machinations,'' Cord interjected in his deep voice, ''don't you think that if I'd wanted to leap straight from your bed to Sheila's, I would have gone to her room rather than my own, or at least have locked my door on the outside chance that you might have come looking for me?''

Ashley smothered a groan because she'd just been asking herself those same questions, only Cord's mind worked faster and he'd posed them before she could.

She turned to him. "If what you've just told me about Sheila is true, then that means she's not only a liar, she's *evil*."

An intensely relieved sound came out of Cord, much like cloth being shredded against the grain. "I came to that conclusion about Sheila the night I found her and my father together."

He stared at her for a long moment. "So, Ash…it seems we're down to her word against mine. Whom do you believe? Has so much damage happened, you can't take my side on any issue? Is *that* the prob—"

But she didn't hear the rest of his question because an aide poked his head in the door. "Lunch is almost over. You'd better hurry down if you want some."

While Cord assured him they'd be right there, Ashley glanced at her watch. It was twenty after twelve. While they'd been reliving the trauma of the past, time had escaped them completely.

"Let's go," Cord muttered, cupping her elbow. "I think the three of us could stand some nourishment about now."

The three of us.

As Cord escorted her down the hall, Ashley had to admit that even if he'd only found out he was going to be a father five hours ago, their baby was already as much a part of his life as it was hers.

When they entered the makeshift dining room, the five other couples greeted them, urging them to join the group. Ashley accepted with an eagerness that she knew irritated Cord.

He wanted an answer from her, but she was still trying to assimilate everything he'd told her and couldn't possibly give him one yet. In Ashley's mind, the subject of Sheila was still very painful. And though Cord's stepmother presented the greatest stumbling block to their happiness, there were other contributing factors they hadn't touched on.

Right now Ashley was thankful for the respite, for other people. She filled her plate with fresh fruit and a roll. Cord made himself a couple of sandwiches out of the cold cuts left and took a liberal helping of salad.

While Cord poured himself a cup of coffee, she sat down with the others and started getting acquainted. He joined her and before long had everyone talking, even the older couple, Kathy and Jerry, who'd at first seemed reticent to contribute. Cord's urbane charm and sophistication was potent.

She passed on the pie, but noticed he had two helpings. Jerry made the comment that being deprived of cigarettes would probably cause them to gain weight in the hospital. His comment brought good-natured laughter from the others. Even Cord's lips curved upward.

It had been so long since Ashley had seen that carefree light in his eyes, she'd almost forgotten how ruggedly handsome he could look. A blush crept over her face and neck when he caught her staring at him.

Just then Dr. Drake came in and announced they were going to enjoy a little time getting acquainted as a group, learning about each other's families, children, hobbies, interests,

"Are you ready?" Cord murmured, his tone husky. He only sounded like that when his emotions were affected like hers.

She nodded and looked away, conscious of his arm brushing against her back after he'd helped arrange the chairs in a circle. Their close proximity had the effect of blurring the lines, lowering all her pitiful defenses against his virile appeal.

During the next hour while everyone had the opportunity to express him or herself, Ashley's bones had become liquefied. While they'd been seated, Cord slid his arm around her shoulders, almost as if he couldn't help himself. But because he was a man who had always been physically possessive of her, he probably wasn't aware of the gesture.

Secretly, Ashley had always loved the feeling of being treated as his exclusive property. It made her feel cherished, like she belonged. Maybe it was because she hadn't grown up in a family with loving parents where she knew she was safe and secure.

Whatever the reason, Cord had fulfilled that need in her from the start. If the truth be known, throughout their long separation she'd ached for this closeness. Even more startling was the fact that since he'd dragged her into the housekeeping closet, she found that her craving for his touch had intensified to a feverish pitch.

The group therapy session, presided over by the clinic staff, was the beginning of many they would see throughout the week. Though she imagined Cord was taking everything in, Ashley couldn't concentrate. Her thoughts had been centered on the those first four rapturous years of living with Cord.

Close and compatible on every level, their marriage had been an extremely physical one, as well. Everything had been so perfect until they were told they might never conceive.

Cord changed after that, became more aloof and introspective. During the last two years, they'd stopped sharing. With the advent of Sheila came the death sentence of their marriage.

But he has denied that an affair with Sheila ever happened!

More than anything in the world Ashley wanted to believe him. But it was still difficult to understand how any woman could do that to another woman—how Sheila would dare tamper with something as sacred as another couple's marriage. Such destructive behavior was anathema to her.

However there was one reality Ashley couldn't deny. Whether Cord had encouraged her or not, Sheila had to be a very unbalanced manipulative person to pursue both him and his father. The more she reviewed it in her mind, the more she couldn't ignore the obvious. Which left her with only one truth. *Cord's truth.*

She buried her head in her hands. He could have no idea how much she wanted to give him the benefit of the doubt. But it would mean placing her heart and soul in his keeping once more. *Full trust.*

Could she do it again, even if they managed to straighten out the other huge problem besetting their marriage?

"What's wrong, Ashley?" he whispered.

The alarm in Cord's voice brought her head around. "Nothing. I—I was just resting my eyes." It was a pitiful excuse, but the only one that came readily to mind.

"Like hell you were." His voice rasped. "You shouldn't be here at this stage in your pregnancy. I'm going to tell Dr. Drake that we're withdrawing. It still might not be too late for someone else to take our place.''

''No, Cord! Don't! I'm perfectly healthy and am planning to see this week through. If you call him, then I'm going to think that you aren't really serious about being in here.''

She saw his chest rise and fall, evidence of the control he was exerting not to contradict her.

''I'm damned either way, aren't I?'' The purely rhetorical question said in such a defeated tone didn't sound as if it were meant for her ears. It brought on an unwelcome spasm of guilt.

''Cord—'' she murmured his name tentatively. ''Please—let's just go back to the room and finish today's interview with Vince.''

Without waiting for a response she left her seat and started for the door to the hall. Cord followed a few steps behind. Since their meeting in the corridor early that morning, this was the first time she'd felt bereft because he didn't try to take her arm or put his hand on her back.

By the time they'd both freshened up, Vince reappeared with a smile. ''Are you two ready to go to work?''

Cord was standing near the window, looking out at the view. When he didn't say anything, Ashley felt compelled to speak. "Yes, of course." In a jerky movement she lowered herself to the edge of the bed, her back to Cord.

Vince pulled up a chair and sat down, once again taking out his legal pad.

"This afternoon we'll concentrate on you, Ashley. How old are you?"

"Twenty-nine."

"Tell me about your family and schooling."

"I was given to an orphanage by my fifteen-year-old unwed mother. I grew up at St. Anne's here in Salt Lake and was placed in several foster homes until I turned eighteen. By that period in my life I had a full-time job waitressing at a restaurant near the university.

"With the money I earned, I went to night school and lived in a campus dorm. Because it cost so much, it took me six years to graduate in accounting."

"Good for you. What jobs did you do after that?"

"I didn't get a job in my field right away, so I moved into an apartment with three other girls and kept on waitressing. About six months later I was hired by Pier Ten Imports to do accounting at the main office in Salt Lake.''

''How did you meet Cord?''

''All of us at the apartment wanted to take a vacation together. So we planned and saved money for a week's trip to the Tetons. While we were staying at the Jackson Lake Lodge, we heard you could climb the Grand Teton mountain and thought we'd try it.

''On our way up, one of those huge summer squalls caught us by surprise. It was quite terrifying, so we decided we'd better go back. On the way down, one of the girls fell and broke her ankle. I stayed with her while the others went for help. Cord and another ranger came to our rescue.''

''Was it love at first sight?'' He winked.

''Yes,'' she admitted quietly. Ashley was thankful she couldn't see Cord's face right now.

''Did you marry soon after?''

''Yes. At a church in Jackson Hole.''

''You had no idea your husband had ever had a smoking habit?''

"No. He was so strong and fit and relaxed, I simply can't picture Cord lighting up a cigarette. I guess I'm still in shock."

"Would you characterize your marriage as happy?"

She struggled for breath. "Every day I woke up so happy I was married to Cord, I couldn't believe it. Sometimes it terrified me that our relationship seemed too perfect. I was afraid it wasn't real, that I might be dreaming and wake up without him."

"When did it start to go wrong?"

"After we'd been married for about two years, we tried to have a baby. When a whole year went by and nothing happened, I visited an obstetrician in Salt Lake to see if there was anything wrong. He said everything looked good. To relax. If I didn't conceive within the next six months, he told me to come in again and bring Cord.

"Well, nothing happened, so we made an appointment for the both of us. That's when we found out Cord had a problem that meant it was almost impossible for me to get pregnant. The odds were definitely not in our favor."

"Did you talk about adopting a baby?"

"No," she whispered in remembered agony.

Vince looked perplexed. "Why?"

"I wanted to—" she blurted. "You can't imagine how much. But I was waiting for Cord to broach the subject first because I knew how devasta—"

"Let's talk about devastation, shall we?" Cord broke in without hesitation, cutting her off. She jerked around on the bed. His face held a pallor that hadn't been there at lunch. "If you could have seen the look in your eyes, Ashley, you would have known why I didn't dare bring up the idea of adoption." His voice rasped.

She was aghast. "What look? What are you talking about?"

Unexpectedly Vince rose to his feet and looked at both of them. "I think I've done enough probing for today. You've touched on a sensitive issue which has obviously strained your marriage. I'm going to leave you to your privacy, and I'll be back tomorrow morning at eight.

"In the meantime, you are welcome to go for walks on this floor and use the facilities in the gym and Jacuzzi pool at the south end of the hall. Someone from the staff will be there at all times for support. After dinner at six, you'll be free to watch movies in the auditorium or enjoy television."

"Vince?" Ashley caught up with him outside the room, wishing he wouldn't have left so abruptly. She didn't think she was ready for the next confrontation with Cord.

"Yes, Ashley?"

"I know we're not supposed to leave the hospital for any reason, but I thought I'd better tell you I have a doctor's appointment on Wednesday."

"As long as you and your husband go together, I don't see a problem. But to be on the safe side, I'll inform Dr. Drake."

"Thank you."

Everything was growing more complicated. Her obstetrican, Dr. Noble, had never said a word when she told him she was getting a divorce, but she knew deep down he disapproved. When he saw Cord in his office, not only would he be surprised and pleased, he'd assume they were back together. Nothing could be further from the truth.

Ashley shivered in apprehension and went back inside the room. Cord had shed his suit and tie. The sleeves of his pale blue shirt had been rolled up to the elbows and he'd undone the top buttons. She caught him tucking the ends inside the waistband of his jeans. Dressed informally, he looked more like the Cord of old, before he'd had to take over the reins of the McKnight Company. He had a hunted, lean look, but for all that he was the most attractive man she'd ever met.

He lounged negligently against the wall near the window, his arms folded across his broad chest. "I understood there were to be no secrets while we were in here."

Ashley came to a standstill. "I was asking Vince what to do about my doctor's appointment on Wednesday. As far as he knows, it's all right for both of us to go."

She sensed the instant his body stopped being relaxed. "Dr. Noble *does* know I'm the father?" His acid tone wounded her.

"Of course he does, Cord. I have no doubt he's been wanting to congratulate you for a long time. He's told me repeatedly that he considers our pregnancy a miracle.''

''It *is*,'' came the thick reply. ''I still can't believe my own eyes.''

''At first I was incredulous, too. But as time went on and I could no longer lie on my stomach, I began to believe a baby was growing inside me.''

''You always did prefer that position when you wanted to go to sleep.'' He made a step toward her. ''I've missed having *you* for a blanket.''

The intimate pictures those words conjured up sent a wave of heat through her body. ''Cord—I—I think th—''

''It's been a long time, hasn't it, Ashley?'' he broke in, not sounding the least repentant. ''Long enough that you're uncomfortable remembering how it was with us. Let me refresh your memory.''

Before she could guess his intentions, he'd slid his hands around her neck.

''Please don't do that,'' she begged when she felt his thumbs slowly caress the pulse hammering at her throat. He was so much taller and stronger than she was. His male aura seemed to engulf her senses.

"Then perhaps you'd prefer *this*—"

Suddenly she was in his arms, their baby imprinted against him as he lowered his head and covered her mouth with his own.

"No, Cord—" Her words slurred as she fought him, but there was something so intimate and sensual about the feel of his hard body against her protruding stomach, she couldn't prevent a gasp escaping. It was all he needed to deepen their kiss.

Caught off guard, Ashley found herself responding with a hunger equal to his.

"I've never stopped wanting you," he confessed on a ragged whisper. She could feel his hands roaming her back in that old familiar way, fanning the heat that was already starting to burn out of control.

"To think my baby is inside here." There was an ache in his voice before she felt one of his hands move around to her stomach and press softly in different places.

"I want to see you, see what I've done to you." He mouthed the words against her lips. Suddenly the tie at her neck was undone. "I want to behold my wife and child. I want to inspect every beautiful inch. Help me, darling.''

By now it was impossible to tell who was trembling the most as his hands started to gather the material of her dress and raise it over her head.

At the last second sanity returned and Ashley tore her lips from his. ''We can't do this, Cord—'' she cried and backed away, but he still held on to the hem of her dress.

His half-smile was mysterious and compelling. When he was like this, she didn't have a rational thought in her head.

''I'll put a do not disturb sign outside the door. No one will bother us if that's what you're worried about. This program is for married couples and we've got the rest of the afternoon to ourselves.''

In panic, Ashley tried to put more distance between them, but he wouldn't let her go. His eyes had darkened with desire. She knew that look and her mouth went dry.

In a deep voice he murmured, ''You want me as much as I want you, Ashley. I can feel it with every heartbeat.''

Her cheeks were on fire. "I don't deny it." Her voice shook. "But making love instead of resolving our problems is the reason we're getting a divorce, Cord. Or have you forgotten!"

The reminder of why they were here worked its magic. That blaze of raw hunger in his eyes vanished and he slowly let the material fall from his hands. A part of her died a little more in the process.

"I've forgotten nothing," he ground out quietly. "Especially not the way I felt when I found out I couldn't give you a child. You could have no idea of the pain I experienced when I realized I wouldn't be able to do the one thing for you that you wanted and needed most in life."

"But that's crazy!" she shot back in consternation. "*You* were all I ever wanted or needed. Cord—you were my whole life!"

The entire room reverberated with her declaration, but he continued to stand there shaking his head.

"No. Do you think I didn't know the pain you suffered being raised in an orphanage with no family to care for you? Do you think I didn't understand how painful it was for you when you realized you'd married half a man? One who couldn't give you a baby of your own?'' The tormented expression on his face crucified her.

"But, Cord—''

"Being my wife condemned you to more of the same hell you'd had to put up with all your life. I lived in terror that you'd leave me as soon as we were given the bad news. I was afraid to mention adoption for fear it would revolt you and drive you away sooner!''

"*Drive me away*—''

Revolt me? She couldn't comprehend what he was telling her.

"Come on, Ashley,'' he bit out tormentedly. "Let's not pretend you didn't want to leave. There are no words to describe how inadequate I felt, how emasculated. Any day I expected you to tell me you wanted a divorce. It killed me because I knew I had no right to hold on to you if you asked for one.''

She stared at him in profound disbelief. "*That's* the reason you became so aloof and withdrawn?''

"Why else?" His voice throbbed with emotion.

She clung to the chair back. "Wherever did you get the idea that a baby was more important than you? Don't you realize that *you* were my family? My *everything*! If we couldn't have children, it didn't matter. I was blissfully happy with you, Cord."

"The only reason I didn't bring up adoption to you at first was because I knew how disappointed you were, Ashley. Here we'd talked about having a big family, and then to find out I couldn't get you pregnant. Sheila told me I should give you time to get over the blow."

"*Sheila* said that?" Ashley cried out angrily. "Oh, Cord— Don't you see how she manipulated us? I thought you couldn't bring yourself to raise a child that wasn't your own flesh and blood. Then I began to have other thoughts. Like the fact that because you and your father were estranged, you decided it might be better not to have children at all, and avoid more pain."

His features tautened. "The relationship with my father had absolutely nothing to do with anything. You deserved a husband who could give you a houseful of children. After we met, one of the first things you told me was that having a family of your own was all you would ever ask of life.

"When it became clear that I couldn't provide that for you, I waited for you to come and tell me you wanted out of our marriage."

Tears stung her eyes. "While you were waiting, I mistook your reticence for indifference. In time, I suspected you'd fallen out of love with me. I no longer knew how to reach you.

"On those visits we took to Salt Lake to visit Greg and Bonnie, and stop by your father's home, you seemed more interested in talking to Sheila about business than sharing with me. Because she indicated the two of you went back a long way—which is something you never intimated to me—I came to the conclusion that you must still care about her. It sickened me and broke my heart."

A dark frown marred his handsome features. "I was wrong not to have told you about Sheila. I was wrong about a lot of things," he confessed on a half-groan.

She lifted her tormented gaze to his. "That's the problem with us, Cord. We did too many things wrong, made too many wrong assumptions. In the process, we destroyed each other."

"Not quite," he came back sharply. "We created a baby together. We did *that* part right."

So saying, he grabbed a pair of shorts from one of the drawers and headed for the door, then paused.

"I'm going to the gym, but before I walk out of here there's something you should know. Now that I realize I'm going to be a father, I'm phoning my attorney to call off the divorce. If you want to fight it, go ahead, but you'll have to obtain it over my dead body and I don't plan to give up the ghost for at least a half a century!"

CHAPTER FIVE

IT HAD *happened.*

The thing she'd worried about had happened. The news that they were expecting a baby had changed everything. Cord meant what he said. He'd fight her on the divorce. With his money, he could afford to keep their case deadlocked for months. *Even years*, she supposed.

Ashley realized he was upset and had walked out on her just now to cool off before they said anything more hurtful. But she was upset, too, and hated it when he deserted her so abruptly, leaving her an emotional wreck.

There was still another issue they hadn't touched on. A big one. But she couldn't very well follow him and get into another discussion when other people would probably be in there using the equipment and could hear every word. Cord was counting on that. No wonder he'd purposely chosen a public place which would make a private talk impossible.

At a totally loose end, she walked over to the closet, reached for the large sewing bag Cord had put away for her and sat down on the chair again, relieved to have something to do with her hands.

The ladies at the church near Mrs. Bromwell's apartment held a homemaking session every Wednesday night and had helped her get started on a quilt for her baby.

The white, silky material was a washable whipped-cream crepe which would be soft against an infant's skin. Once the adorable lamb pattern had been stenciled on the fabric and she'd been taught how to make those tiny, perfect stitches and knots, Ashley had done most of the quilting herself. Now that it had been taken off the frames, she needed to bind it and had chosen a white lace eyelet for the trim.

Soon she would be able to wrap her new baby inside it. That day wasn't very far off. There was a lot to be done to get ready. At least she could finish the quilt before she left the hospital.

It made her sad that she knew nothing about her own mother, who had only been a girl when she'd had Ashley. The nuns had no memento, no picture to show her. For that matter, Ashley knew absolutely nothing about her father. He'd probably been a teenager, too. Most likely both of them were alive and married with other children of their own.

Early in their courtship Cord had offered to hire a private investigator to find her parents. Though Ashley adored him for it, she'd told him no. She preferred living with the fantasies she'd woven about her origins. The nuns had been kind to her, had taught her to rely on God and her good mind to get her through life. Then she had had Cord and she'd needed nothing else.

That formula had worked until Cord had found out he couldn't give her a child. That's when the real trauma of life began...

While she hand-sewed the lace inserted between the quilt edges, she determined that her own baby would never suffer the same fate. Though Ashley couldn't see her and Cord getting back together—not when there was too much painful history between them—he would play a loving, vital role in their son's or daughter's life, just as Ashley determined to be the best mother on earth.

Cord wouldn't like the furnished apartment she'd put a first month's deposit on, but it was clean and quite bright for a basement. The widow who lived in the upstairs portion of the house seemed like she'd be a nice landlady. She welcomed a baby. It was teenagers with loud music she didn't want living below. Above all, she wouldn't tolerate smokers or drinkers for tenants.

Ashley felt fortunate to have found a place to live in a decent neighborhood. She could park her car off the street at the back of the house where she could go down the steps to her own apartment which was tiny. The crib she hadn't purchased yet would have to fit right next to her bed.

She'd bathe her baby on the counter at the kitchen sink. The nuns always bathed the foundling babies in the orphanage's kitchen sink. When Ashley was old enough, she'd been given the job. Taking care of babies was a joy.

Not every girl in the orphanage cared about babies, but Ashley was happiest when she was given that task rather than washing dishes or doing laundry for twenty or so residents. Many were the nights she'd helped the sisters nurse a child with colic or croup.

The experience had prepared her for motherhood. She didn't feel the least bit nervous about giving her baby physical care. It was her son or daughter's emotional well-being Ashley worried about. She didn't want her problems with Cord to put a blight on their child's happiness.

Because of Cord's estrangement from his father, a man Ashley had only met twice before his death, she was certain that Cord would do everything in his power to be the best parent he could. Even if they lived apart, between the two of them, they would find a way to fill their child's physical and emotional needs.

Ignoring a nagging voice that told her living separate lives would not make for a contented son or daughter, Ashley worked faster at her handiwork. As a result, she held herself too rigidly. Before long her back started aching.

With a deep sigh she got up from the chair, left the quilt and lace on the seat, then lay down on her side on top of the bed. She only intended to rest for a few minutes, then get up and sew some more.

At some point she must have fallen asleep and knew nothing until she felt the small of her back being massaged with exquisite tenderness by a hand that seemed to know exactly where and how to apply the right pressure.

The feeling was so delightful, at first she thought she was dreaming and lay there in a warm, semiconscious condition as delicious sensations spread throughout her body, even to her fingertips.

The baby was moving in her womb, almost as if it were trying to find its favorite position, but couldn't quite decide which one it liked best.

In her trancelike condition, she scarcely registered the fact that the source of her pleasure had left her back and was now freely roaming her stomach, absorbing the movement of the life growing inside her.

"Dear God, Ashley—" she heard a deep, familiar male voice murmur in awe.

Her eyes flew open.

She was no longer alone on the bed. Cord lay behind her, his right arm pillowing her head, his left hand getting to know their unborn child. There was no space separating them. She felt the warmth of his hard-muscled body from the back of her head to the back of her knees and all the way to her nylon-clad feet where his stocking feet tangled with hers.

Attempting to get up, she discovered she was trapped. "Don't move yet," he begged. "When I lie next to you like this, I can feel the baby's restlessness and almost imagine it's a physical part of me, too. The motions are so strong, I think it must be a boy."

She swallowed hard. "I—I think it is, too," she whispered. His nearness made it difficult to talk normally.

"Have you thought of a name for him?" he murmured into her hair, his lips lingering against the curve of her neck.

Her body shivered in ecstatic reaction. "Because of your name, I was thinking of having him christened Cabe. It's Scottish, like yours."

"I like it." She could hear him smiling. Her suggestion had pleased him. "Very much in fact," he murmured playfully. The low tones vibrated through her entire nervous system, almost as if their bodies were linked by some mystical force. "But if it's a girl, I want to call her Mary-Ashley."

She blinked in astonishment. "Why?"

"Because you once told me that one of the nuns you loved had secretly nicknamed you Sister Mary-Ashley in the hopes that you'd grow up and find your vocation as a nun.

"*Thank God* you didn't, but the name is beautiful, *just like you*." His voice trailed off. His arm slid all the way around her stomach and he held her even closer, if that was possible.

In panic she blurted, "I need to get up and use the rest room."

Instead of a protest, a chuckle met her outcry. "I've heard a pregnant woman can never afford to be too far from a bathroom, especially during the last few months."

She inhaled a huge lungful of air as he released her and helped her to sit up. She braced herself to get off the bed. "I swear there's absolutely no more room inside me. I can't even imagine what I'm going to look like in another couple of weeks."

If they could keep things light when they were alone, she just might survive the rest of the week.

He levered himself behind her, putting his hands to her shoulders once they were both on their feet. ''I'm sorry about your discomfort. But if you want to know the truth, after thinking we couldn't have our own child, I can't imagine anything more beautiful than the sight of you nine months' pregnant.''

With another breathtaking kiss to the side of her neck, he let her go. Her body was shaking so hard, she could barely walk to the bathroom door unaided. Cord could have no idea of his effect on her senses.

''We're going to be late for dinner,'' he said as soon as she emerged a few minutes later.

A hand went to her throat. ''I can't believe I slept so long. Did you enjoy your workout at the gym?''

His half-smile tugged at her heart. ''Very much. Most of the guys on the program were in there. They all envied me my gorgeous roommate and wondered where I found the time to smoke when I had a wife like you waiting for me down the hall.''

She averted her eyes as heat filled her cheeks. Inwardly she moaned because all the old feelings for him which had been lying dormant had come to life once more. He was acting exactly like the Cord she'd fallen in love with. It simply wasn't fair.

''After that comment, I didn't last long because all I could think about was getting back to the room. To *you*,'' he said in a husky voice. ''When I discovered that you were in a deep sleep, I decided I could use a nap myself.

''Though I have a perfectly good hospital bed of my own not six feet away from you, I admit that I took advantage of your vulnerable state. In truth, I couldn't help myself and refuse to apologize.''

Unrepentant and self-confident, he escorted her to the dining room where she had to face all those married men who had shared some private thoughts and moments together in the gym. She knew all was said in fun.

Nevertheless she blushed once more when she entered the room with Cord's arm around her shoulders because one of them winked at Cord in greeting.

Fortunately the women appeared to be in a talkative mood. They wanted to know how soon Ashley was due. The conversation centered around children and before long the whole group was sharing pictures of their own children and in some cases, grandchildren.

Every woman in the room had been a mother, so each one had a tale to tell of their delivery which was embellished by their husbands until all were laughing.

It felt good. Six couples, all bonded together because of a desire to make a change for the better in their lives. They shared stories and talked as if they'd been close friends for years. But eventually, the talk got around to the reason why they were all in the hospital.

At that point, Cord's pleasant, almost lazily satisfied demeanor changed. The hand holding hers tightened into a fierce grip before he seemed to realize what he was doing and let it go with a low-murmured apology.

When they returned to their room Cord took her by the shoulders and stared down into her eyes, his expression sober.

''I can't promise yet that I won't smoke another cigarette in my lifetime, but I swear to you right now that I'll never, ever smoke around you or our child.'' His voice rang with conviction.

Her eyes smarted, but she didn't look away. ''I believe you, Cord. There's no question in my mind that you're going to be a loving, caring, demonstrative father, that you'll be all the things your own father missed being.

''Since we both recognize that this child's conception was nothing less than miraculous, I *know*,'' her voice shook, ''that you'll keep your promise.''

His eyes were hooded as he whispered, ''Thank you for that.'' He unexpectedly lowered his head and brushed her lips with his. A featherlight kiss which felt like the seal of a vow, rather than a prelude to passion. She had the overwhelming conviction in her heart that he would never break that vow. She loved him for it.

''While you get ready for bed, I'll set up Boggle.''

''*Boggle*?'' It was a spelling game they often played on snowy winter nights at the ranger's cabin after they were married. Just the mention of it brought back myraid memories that made her heart turn over. "Did you find it in the lounge?"

He flashed her one of his heart-stopping smiles. "No. I brought it from home in the hope that you'd play it with me."

It had been on the tip of her tongue to refuse him on the grounds that she was too tired. But secretly, she was afraid to spend any more time with him.

Every conceivable barrier which she'd taken the greatest pains to erect in order to counteract his power, was in danger of being knocked aside by an unexpected look of desire igniting his dark blue eyes, or the compelling curve of his male mouth at a vulnerable moment.

But the therapy had to be working, because she didn't have the heart to turn him down. In all honesty, after eight months' deprivation, she craved every moment with him.

"All right. I'll change and be with you in a minute."

Without glancing at him, she hurried over to the drawers and drew out the things she needed, but one item was missing.

"I hung your robe on the bathroom door." He read her mind, just like he used to do.

"Thank you," she said and quietly slipped into the bathroom, her pulse beating far too fast to be healthy. *Heavens*! She felt much more shy than she had on her wedding night.

How many times had they made love during their six-year marriage? At least several thousand anyway. They were expecting a baby, yet she could easily be that same virginal bride who was anticipating their wedding night with all that excitement and maidenly fears that were part of her heritage being brought up by nuns.

Tortured by the nature of her thoughts, she showered and prepared for bed, praying that Cord might have started watching a show on TV while he waited for her. Hopefully he'd be too engrossed to care about a game and she could go right to sleep.

But she'd forgotten that he disliked television except for some of the nature films. He preferred reading the newspaper to watching the news which he claimed didn't give the true story on anything. She happened to share his opinion.

When they'd lived in the Tetons, they didn't bother to buy a TV set. They both read a lot of books. But mostly they talked about what they'd done during the day while they made dinner and did the dishes together.

Afterward they'd play games, or put on music and dance. Later, they made passionate love. Those years had been so idyllic, maybe she shouldn't have expected life to go on like that.

When she tiptoed from the bathroom wearing the yellow crushed-nylon robe which would barely fit by the time she delivered, there was no sound from the TV to greet her ears.

Instead, Cord had changed into his green robe and was sitting next to her bed, the Boggle box in his hand.

Don't think about the last time you saw that robe, Ashley, or it will tear you apart all over again.

Cord glanced in her direction. She felt his probing gaze linger on the outline of her body before he patted the mattress. He might as well have been touching her. "Come on and get in. We'll use this side of the bed for a table."

Ashley walked around the end of the bed and got in as gracefully as she could, but it was a terrible struggle to remain dignified. "Don't you dare laugh at me," she snapped when she noticed his mouth quirk. Inching her way until she was lying on her side facing him, the covers reaching her chin, she added, "A man will never know what it's like to resemble an overgrown tuna who can't get around without being hoisted."

As he adjusted the pillows for her, a low bark of male laughter burst forth, its sound thrilling her in spite of her efforts not to be affected by him.

"You could never look like a tuna, darling." But there was a distinct twinkle in those blue depths that told her he could see her as something else.

"A plump partridge then?" she prodded.

His smile broadened. "I'm in enough trouble with you as it is, so I plead the fifth out of self-preservation."

His words, tossed in the air during a moment of funning, found an unwitting target.

Before she lost her courage she said, "Tell me something, Cord—"

"Anything," he came back so fiercely, she realized that all levity had ceased for him, as well.

She bit her lip. "When you saw that I was pregnant, why did you assume it was Greg's baby?"

Lines darkened his handsome features. "When I passed you in the hall, it took me a second to realize that it *was* you."

His eyes searched hers. "You knew how much I loved your long hair." His voice grated. "I figured you would never have cut it unless you'd done it for another man. In my gut I knew you hadn't slept with Greg, but I was so eaten up with pain and jealousy, I said it to make you mad enough to reveal the true father's name."

Another wave of guilt assailed her. "I—I'm sorry you had to find out about the pregnancy the way you did. With hindsight, I can see that keeping it from you was the wrong thing to do," she whispered. "You had every right to know about it as soon as I did." Her voice caught.

"As far as my hair, you have to understand that growing up, I thought I would become a nun. Sister Bernice said I would have to have it all cut off if I joined an order, so I decided I would always keep it long until that day arrived.

"Obviously I passed out of that phase by my senior year in high school, but my hair remained the same length. When I discovered I was pregnant, I had the usual morning sickness and felt hot all the time. That's when the idea came to cut it short. It wasn't done to hurt or shock you on purpose, Cord."

"I realize that," he admitted in thick tones.

"It's just that after all these years, it was fun to try something new and I thought it would be easier to take care of with a baby. But I know I look very different now."

"Do you honestly think your hairstyle makes any difference to me?" he bit out. "Hell, Ashley, you look beautiful either way. As for regrets, I have too many of my own to reproach you for anything. You're carrying my child and you're both healthy. Everything else fades into insignificance."

She nodded. "I agree. Our baby has to come first now."

"Where do you live these days?" His question brought up a whole new subject, one she'd been hesitant to broach because of his inevitable, negative reaction.

She stared at the opposite wall. "I've been staying with an elderly woman, taking care of her, but I ended that job to come into the hospital. When I leave here on Sunday, I'll be living in an apartment in a nice residential area."

A tension-filled silence pervaded the room. "How will you earn your living?"

"I'll be all right for a few months, then I'll find another caretaker position where I can live in with the baby. Mrs. Bromwell and her family will provide me with a good reference."

By now she had expected Cord to interrupt or give her an ultimatum. Earlier he'd told her he wouldn't give her a divorce, yet he was silent on the subject now.

At the least she thought he would demand that she start accepting his money to help take care of additional expenses. It shocked her when he did none of those things. In fact, he said nothing at all.

Admit that it hurts, Ashley. Admit that you were hoping he would put up a fight.

She turned her head in his direction, only to discover him examining the quilt she'd left on the other chair.

"This is beautiful," he marveled before darting her an unreadable glance. "I had no idea you knew how to do this kind of work."

"Some ladies at the church I attend taught me how to quilt."

"We'll have our baby christened in it. Have you bought a special gown?"

Oh, Cord. If only you knew. I haven't bought anything.

"No." Her voice wobbled. "Not yet."

"If you'd rather work on this than play a game, I'll understand."

"No. It's almost finished. I can do it any time this week."

She watched him put it back. His stillness alerted her that he was deep in thought about something earthshaking.

"I'm ready for a round of Boggle whenever you are." she spoke softly to remind him she was still in the room.

"Ashley—if you don't mind, I think I'll pass on the game. Maybe what I need is a cup of coffee. I'm going to walk down to the lounge. Shall I turn out the lights for you?"

Her dejection at the thought of him leaving her alone was greater than she could believe.

"Yes, please."

"Goodnight, Ashley. I'll see you in the morning."

Hot tears trickled from her eyes as she heard the door close behind him. Was his sudden need to get out of the room due to his going a whole day without a cigarette, or was there a lot more to it than that?

She had no idea what he was thinking and feeling. Always at the back of her mind lurked Sheila. Like a malevolent specter, the image of her wearing Cord's robe haunted Ashley.

But Cord swore that there'd been no illicit liaison, that he'd been outside and had no idea Sheila had gone to his room. In front of Vince he'd claimed to *despise* his stepmother.

It's my word against hers, Ashley. Whom are you going to believe?

The question went 'round and 'round in her head. Had he grown tired of asking it?

Is that why he'd walked out just now? Because she'd told him her plans after she left the hospital on Sunday, and what she'd said had let him know that she didn't intend to live with him again?

He would translate that to mean she didn't believe him and couldn't forgive him. So why bother anymore…

Could she really blame him when even now she was fighting the fear that he might be calling Sheila?

Why did you leave me just now, Cord? Why are you so silent?

When she thought about it, he'd cared enough to make the initial call to her last Friday. Though their conversation had degenerated before she'd found out the exact favor he'd wanted from her, through further illumination from Greg, she was here now.

All day she and Cord had been communicating the way they once did when they'd been happily married. They'd made a lot of progress today. To have come this far, only for him to go all quiet and retreat within himself where she couldn't reach him, made her want to weep from frustration. It didn't make sense!

It was like déjà vu.

Only this time it was Cord who was running away instead of Ashley. Before this night ended, she planned to confront him, otherwise the whole purpose of this program was wasted on them.

Forgetting her pregnancy, she shot up in bed. The constricting muscles beneath her stomach made her cry out in pain. When they subsided, she removed the covers and carefully got down from the mattress.

A trip to the bathroom to run a brush through her hair and put on some lipstick, and she was ready. The hospital provided slippers which she put on her feet before leaving the room.

With her heart pounding too fast, she padded down to the lounge and opened the door. Several couples were still in there talking, but there was no sign of Cord. They invited her to join them. She thanked them, but declined, using the excuse that she was too tired to stay up any longer.

"Have you seen my husband anywhere?"

Jerry nodded. "He came for a cup of coffee and said he needed to make a phone call, but didn't want to disturb you. I told him to go ahead and use the phone in our room. We're in 506.''

''You'll find him in there, honey,'' his wife concurred.

Her heart plummeted to her feet. ''Thank you.''

Determined as she'd never been in her life, Ashley wheeled out of the lounge and went in search of Cord. Without knocking on the door which had been left ajar, she simply walked in.

Cord stood at the bedside table, the phone to his ear. When he saw who had entered the room, he looked stunned. His dark brows furrowed before he muttered something unintelligible into the receiver, then covered the mouthpiece.

''Ashley? What's wrong?'' There was alarm in his voice.

She sucked in her breath. ''That's what I came to ask you. Who are you talking to?''

''Greg. I was thanking him.''

''For what?''

"For not letting me give up on you. I wanted him to know that the counseling is working."

Her body went rigid. "Aren't you being a little premature? Tonight you closed up on me. After you asked me questions, you didn't let me know what you were thinking. Instead you left the room without saying anything. It's a pattern of yours that helped drive us apart a long time ago.

"I've been as guilty as you in that regard, but I thought the purpose of this program was to change that pattern. Today I answered all your questions as honestly as I could and told you my feelings. I thought we'd achieved a breakthrough of sorts."

Even though she knew Greg was still on the phone—or maybe it was Sheila. Would she ever really know? Now that she'd gotten started, she couldn't seem to stop.

"Just tell me I was wrong, Cord, and we'll end this farce before we waste any more of Dr. Drake's time."

Without as much as a twitch of an eyelid, he raised the receiver to his ear. "Greg— I'll have to call you back."

Somehow she hadn't expected him to act so fast. When he started toward her with purpose in every stride, a frisson of fear attacked her body.

Not wanting an audience, she turned and hurried to their room ahead of him, surprised that she'd had the temerity to approach him while he was still on the phone.

The second he shut the door behind them, he asked in an amazingly calm voice, "How exactly did I shut you out?"

She stood in the center of the room, breathless. "Today you said you would fight me for a divorce. Tonight, you asked me my future plans but made no comment one way or the other. One moment we were going to play a game, the next moment, you disappeared on me.

"What's going on inside you, Cord? If we can't talk about it, then there's no point in our being here."

He folded his arms. "I agree we covered a lot of territory today. Maybe too much for a woman as close to her due date as you. Early this morning Vince warned me to go easy."

''Vince?'' She frowned. ''*He's* the reason you said night-night to me and turned off the lights like I was a little child up past my bedtime?''

''Who else would know I'm like a hot rocket ready to explode off the pad given the slightest encouragement.''

''I'm not sure I understand.''

His eyes flashed dangerously. ''Then I'll explain it to you. You think I like hearing that you have been forced to be a companion to someone else when I should have been waiting on you all this time?

''Instead of going out to lunch with your friends, buying clothes and having showers for the baby, you think I'm thrilled that you've been cooped up with no money, no outlet, no laughter?

''You can forget going back to any apartment after you leave here. You're coming home with me where you belong. We're going to resume wedded life and flaunt our little one-to-be in front of Sheila until she breaks and admits to all the evil she's done. Then we'll both have the pleasure of throwing her out of our house and our lives. Is that enough truth for you?''

CHAPTER SIX

WEDNESDAY turned out to be a beautiful spring day, but maybe that was because Cord went with Ashley for her checkup and she could tell he was excited to be accompanying her.

"Dr. Noble? Before you say anything, I need to explain that Cord didn't know we were expecting until yesterday morning. I—it's my fault," she stammered, unable to sustain Cord's penetrating glance.

Dr. Noble digested her revelation, then said, "Well, Cord. Better late than never. You realize, of course, that you two have defied the odds of having a baby. Congratulations!"

Cord flashed the doctor a quick smile. It tore at Ashley's senses. "I've been in shock since I first caught sight of my very pregnant wife. How is she today?"

"Your blood pressure and iron level are normal. Its heartbeat is perfect."

Cord's thoughtful gaze rested on her once more. "That's good." His voice cracked with emotion.

"Ashley?"

She jerked her head toward the doctor, her heart racing. "You have a good-sized baby in there. Your uterus measures on the high end of the normal range. I can foresee no problems and expect you'll go full term. But to be safe, I'm ordering another ultrasound. Maybe you've changed your mind about wanting to know the baby's gender?"

"She told me she wanted to be surprised," Cord intervened swiftly. "I'll abide by her wishes."

Ashley had trouble swallowing. She was certain Cord was dying to know if they were having a boy or a girl, but so far he'd been totally supportive of her and her desires. It was a very humbling experience. Especially when she had denied him all knowledge of her condition for the last eight months.

She would feel very small if she didn't satisfy his fatherly wishes right now. In truth, she wanted desperately to know if they were having a son or a daughter, but up until today she'd been reticent to hear specifics for fear it would make everything too real.

So far she'd been overwhelmed at the thought of going through the pregnancy and delivery by herself, let alone raising her child as a single mother.

But circumstances had changed. Cord was here. It seemed the right time to share in the news together.

"Actually, we would like to know." The minute the words were out she noticed the abrupt rise and fall of Cord's broad chest.

The doctor's eyes gleamed approvingly. "I'll call downstairs and tell them to fit you in before you leave the clinic today."

If Ashley's heart had been racing before, at this point it was halfway out of her chest cavity. She felt the familiar pressure of Cord's arm as it slid around her shoulders and drew her closer to his hard, masculine body.

He thanked the doctor, sounding as eager as she was, possibly more so because while she'd had over a half a year to absorb the miracle, he was still in the fresh throes of shock at his father-to-be status.

Apparently her doctor could move mountains because within the hour, she was lying on an examining table in a gown, the cold gel rubbed into her skin in preparation.

When her first ultrasound had been taken at eighteen weeks, Ashley had denied herself the pleasure of learning the baby's gender, but she wasn't sorry. To see it with Cord now was perhaps the greatest thrill of her life.

The technician placed the mouselike probe on her stomach. "Keep your eyes on the screen."

Cord pulled up a chair next to her and reached for her hand, kissing her fingertips while he held it firmly in both of his. The gesture melted her bones.

The hormonal changes in her body seemed to heighten her physical awareness of him, even when there was no contact. After such a long period of deprivation, to be touching and feeling again seriously threatened her powers of concentration.

A flash on the screen drew her attention. She gasped because the baby's shape was much more developed and recognizable than before.

"*Lord*—" Cord whispered reverently as the technician began moving the probe around her stomach, pointing out arms, hands, fingers. Its head seemed in perfect proportion to its body.

For maybe twenty minutes they marveled at this miracle of creation moving inside her womb. Suddenly Cord cried, "We have a son!" His joy rang throughout the tiny cubicle.

"You sure do." The technician grinned. "This little guy has got all his parts in all the right places."

The moment was so emotional, Ashley let out a muffled sob. Cord leaned over and kissed her quiet. She couldn't be positive but thought she felt tears on his cheeks, as well.

"Cabe it is." He mouthed the words against her lips. "A good, solid name. I think this calls for some shopping after we get out of here."

Ashley could hear his mind working. Now that he knew they were expecting a son, Cord would want to buy him everything. Of course he would have all their purchases sent to the house.

That would be fine if Ashley were living with Cord, but she wasn't.

After she'd interrupted his phone conversation with Greg, Cord had returned to their hospital room and informed her that she was moving back home with him.

The pronouncement had been delivered in the most forbidding tone she'd ever heard him utter. After admonishing her to get a good night's sleep because they had a great deal to accomplish the next day, he'd left her alone.

She could have gone after him right then and insisted that nothing was settled, that it was still his word against Sheila's. But she'd underestimated her husband's desire to keep them a family.

The challenge he'd flung at her about catching Sheila at her own game had been so unexpected and had hit so hard at the root of Ashley's turmoil, she'd needed time to absorb what he'd suggested.

In plain English Cord had said that he expected Ashley to live with him again. Together they would force Sheila's hand and prove her to be the liar Cord had claimed all along. Only in that way could Ashley's hidden fears be stilled once and for all. *Would Cord make that kind of wild suggestion unless he was confident of the outcome?*

Over the last twenty-four hours Ashley had considered all the ramifications of such a plan. Certainly if she didn't go along with it, she would never be able to obtain the indisputable proof for herself. Her heart would always entertain doubts. Cord knew that. He was willing to take the risk.

But was she?

Ashley hadn't honestly known the answer to that question—not until they'd seen the ultrasound where the reality of their baby boy had put things into perspective and had made her realize what she'd be fighting for.

It forced her to understand that if she didn't get to the bottom of her pain and face Sheila, she'd never know another moment's peace. Worst of all, she'd be depriving their son of a home with both father and mother.

Cord wanted another chance. He was doing everything humanly possible to make their marriage work. He'd entered the hospital to rid himself of an addiction. The rest was up to Ashley. But there was someone she needed to talk things over with first, before she committed.

"I—I think it's time I got dressed," she said in a quiet voice, not wanting to discuss their personal lives in front of an audience.

She could tell by Cord's tight-lipped expression that her silence on the subject of going shopping after this visit had upset him. In an ominous gesture he rose to his full height and informed the technician that the two of them needed to get back to City Creek Hospital right away.

Though the older woman looked surprised, she immediately turned off the machine. Cord walked her out of the room, thanking her for fitting them in so quickly. As their voices trailed, Ashley could hear him asking specific questions about the measurements taken.

Ashley took advantage of the time alone to get off the examining table and return to her locker down the hall. Once out of the hospital gown provided by the clinic, she slipped back into the pants and top she'd purchased the weekend before.

When she returned to the reception area, Cord stood there waiting, the look in his eyes watchful and guarded.

"Before we do anything more," she began, "I'd like to stop by St. Anne's. Do you mind?"

If he found her request odd, he didn't comment on it.

"Not at all," he murmured before ushering her out to his cream-colored Land Rover.

They accomplished the short drive to the orphanage in relative silence. Before she could suggest that he wait in the car, he came around to her side and helped her down. Together they climbed the steps of the four-story facility, a dull-red brick building which had been converted into an orphanage after World War I. Except for her college years, Ashley had spent her whole life here and felt a bittersweet twinge as they crossed over the threshold.

A woman Ashley didn't recognize now manned the front desk, but the same smell of disinfectant and boiled cabbage reached her nostrils, bringing back myriad memories.

Thank heaven their son would have his own parents to raise him!

"You go find Sister Bernice." He read her mind. "I'll wait in the reception area."

'I—I won't be long, Cord."

"Take all the time you need," he came back reasonably. "I realize she represents the mother figure in your life."

His astute observation took her back for a moment.

"I'm not going to light up a cigarette in your absence, if that's what you're worried about," he added beneath his breath.

She flinched at the acidity of his remark. "The thought never entered my head. Sister Bernice was very taken with you the first time you were introduced to her before our marriage. I know she'll want to say hello to you before we leave."

He appeared to digest her remark before he said, "Why don't you find her first. If it's convenient, maybe she'll come out to greet me."

Ashley nodded. "I'll be right back." She wheeled around and headed for the office. Though the orphanage was a state-run program, various sisters from the church performed service here.

When Ashley had left Cord's house that fateful morning, she'd run straight to Sister Bernice who was now in charge of St. Anne's. The head nun, most likely in her late sixties, had always been a positive influence in Ashley's life.

After Ashley had left Cord, Sister Bernice had been the one to let her stay at the orphanage in exchange for helping the children. Within two weeks, she'd assisted Ashley to find the job of live-in housekeeper to Mrs. Bromwell.

Ashley owed Sister Bernice a debt of gratitude she could never repay. Since entering the building a few minutes ago, Ashley was even more impressed over the great work the nun had accomplished throughout the years, playing the role of mother, nurse and educator to parentless children, who like Ashley, would have been abandoned to fate.

When she knocked on the door and was told by a familiar voice to enter, her heart swelled within her.

The nun's eyes lit up when she saw who it was. "Ashley, my child. Come in, come in. Sit down."

"You don't mind the intrusion?" she asked, taking a seat opposite the older woman's desk.

"You know me better than that." She shook her head. "How long before the big event?"

"About three weeks now."

"I want to be informed when you go to the hospital. I can't wait to see your little one."

Ashley smiled, fighting tears. "I'll phone you as soon as I can. I want you to be there and hold my baby. You're the closest thing to a grandmother he will ever know."

"*He*, is it?" Sister Bernice chuckled, sounding very pleased at the honor Ashley had accorded her. But then she sobered. "Have you told his father yet?" The older sister knew everything.

"Y-yes."

"*When*?"

"On Monday," she ventured in a guilty tone. Just then Ashley felt about ten years old, when Sister Bernice had caught her out doing something she shouldn't, like taking one of the babies to bed with her and pretending it was her real sister.

Of course that was against the rules. Sister Bernice had only smiled and told Ashley to take the baby back to the nursery, assuring her that one day, Ashley would grow up to have a baby of her own. Until that time, she would have to wait and learn how to be a mother.

"At least he knows," Sister Bernice finally said with a deep sigh. "All right— I can tell you have something important on your mind. I have the time to listen."

Sister Bernice's wisdom and kindness had made her beloved of the children at the orphanage. She hadn't changed over the years. She was still the same wonderful nun who remained pensive and nonjudgmental. This endearing quality made it easy for Ashley to unburden herself.

The older woman sat back in her chair, her palms together beneath her chin as she contemplated everything Ashley had told her. "So now you're nervous about facing your husband's stepmother because she has always intimidated you. I'm not surprised. This Sheila reminds me very much of another child we had here at the orphanage. Do you remember Marsha?"

Marsha.

Just the sound of that name brought back pain.

"Yes," she answered in a trembling voice. "She was the one who finally ran away from St. Anne's..."

"That's right. She was four years older than you, and very jealous of you, Ashley."

Ashley stared dumbfounded at Sister Bernice. "You *knew* that?"

"I noticed. We didn't get her until a certain amount of damage had already been done to her psyche."

When Ashley looked back, she realized that Marsha had done everything in her power to put Ashley in the wrong and get her into trouble. For a young girl, she was amazing cruel and devious. *Like Sheila...*

"But you're a grown-up now. You don't have to be intimidated or frightened by anyone. Your husband's suggestion makes sense. He wants to expose this Sheila for who she really is. If you were to go back to his house and live with him again, you would be provided with the perfect opportunity to see this thing through and discover the truth for yourself."

Ashley took in a huge breath. ''But what if Cord is still hiding things from me?''

Sister Bernice eyed her shrewdly. ''Then it's your duty as his wife to find out, isn't it?''

She hadn't thought of it quite like that. ''Yes.''

''Because you still love him. Otherwise you would never have agreed to join the program at the hospital with him.''

''You're right. I think I love him more than ever,'' she cried softly. ''You should see how excited he is about the baby.''

''As well he should be. Ashley—since you've come to me, I'm going to tell you something. I can *promise* you that you're more than equal to the challenge of facing Sheila or anyone else, *if* you'll do it. Three lives are at stake here. Surely the welfare of a lovely family like yours is worth the fight. You above all people should understand that.''

She bowed her head. ''I do. I guess I just needed to hear you tell me again that you believe in me.''

''Was there ever any doubt?''

''No,'' she whispered emotionally.

"That's my girl. Now let's not keep your husband waiting any longer."

Sister Bernice, a tall regal woman with a smiling face that put everyone at ease, got up from the chair and walked out to the foyer with Ashley. Cord rose to his feet the second he saw them coming.

The nun beamed at him as they shook hands. "Congratulations to the expectant father."

"Thank you, Sister," Cord murmured in a cordial tone. "It's good to see you again."

"I couldn't be more delighted with this visit and am looking forward to holding your child when he's born."

"I'll phone you the moment Ashley delivers," he promised.

"I'll be waiting." Her gray eyes twinkled. "Before you leave here, feel free to step inside the chapel and thank God for the miracle He has bestowed on you. I, too, will say my prayers for you."

Her gaze sent Ashley a private message. Then she made the sign of the cross and walked off, disappearing down another corridor.

Cord studied Ashley's features. "Where is the chapel?" he asked in a voice as deep as velvet.

She cleared her throat. "Through those doors on the right."

By tacit agreement they entered the small, simple room and sat down on the end pew. While Cord leaned forward, his hands clasped, Ashley closed her eyes and offered a prayer of thanksgiving as well as a plea that it wouldn't be a mistake to go back home with him after they left the hospital.

"Ashley?" He spoke once they'd returned to the car and were on the road once more. When he said her name like that, her body tautened nervously.

"Yes?"

"Aside from the quilt you're making, what have you bought for the baby?"

"Nothing yet." It was embarrassing to admit, but because of meager finances and no place to keep things, she'd put that day off. "I was waiting until I moved into the apartm—"

"Which damn well isn't going to happen," he cut her off in a savage tone. "I'll need a phone number so I can call the landlord and tell him to rent it to someone else.''

Ashley trembled. *Cord wants a commitment, and he wants it now.*

''He's a *she*. I'll phone her when we get back to the hospital.''

It wasn't anything tangible, yet she could feel some of the tension leave his body.

''Did you sign a lease?''

''Yes. For six months.''

''I'll take care of it,'' he muttered, then changed gears. ''Since you're coming home with me, why don't we pick out a few things today, and arrange to have them delivered to the house on Monday?''

She tried to imagine Sheila's shock, and couldn't.

''But we don't have a room ready!''

''That will be our first project next week. In the meantime we'll store everything in the spare bedroom next to ours.''

Ours.

She'd never been comfortable in that house, let alone the bedroom, unless Cord had been sharing it with her, of course. But that was all a long time ago. She craved to return to the ranger cabin, to the life which had made both of them so happy.

But that wasn't meant to be, and it was only natural that Cord would want to hold on to the McKnight family home where he'd been born and raised. If memories of his father weren't that pleasant, he *had* loved his mother and would always associate the house with her.

Ashley needed to be more sensitive to his feelings and block the image of Sheila draped across Cord's bed from her mind. Otherwise she'd be crippled with renewed pain.

"Are you too tired to visit a store I have in mind?" Cord prodded.

Though she felt exhausted after wrestling with her emotions, she didn't dare disappoint him. "No, but it is getting close to dinner. We should have been back on the floor before now."

"The ultrasound was more important. We can grab a burger on the way. Right now I want to drive over to Forsey's."

Cord remembered!

A little thrill rippled through her body. Forsey's sold hand-made, nineteenth-century reproductions of all kinds of furniture, specializing in baby cradles, cribs, dressers, tiny rocking chairs and little dollhouses.

Before she and Cord had found out that they probably wouldn't be able to have children, Ashley had prevailed on him to stop at that store every time they'd driven down to Salt Lake from the Tetons.

Since their separation, she'd given up any ideas about owning such expensive furnishings, but obviously Cord hadn't forgotten. He knew she'd always had her heart set on the natural oak pieces. That particular decor would work well in a boy's room.

By the time they'd reached the store and Cord had helped her out of the Land Rover, Ashley was feverish with excitement and anxiety. Though they were the same two people, everything had changed because during their drive from the orphanage, she had agreed to end the separation and live with him again.

In her mind, they still had to work out the details. She'd been sharing a bedroom at the hospital with him, but she wasn't ready to make love. She had a demon to face first.

Unfortunately she feared Cord entertained other ideas. There was a subtle difference in

him as they spent time in the various show-
rooms—a palpable, sensual energy she felt ra-
diate from him whenever he whispered something private in her ear or hugged her waist in
a possessive grip.

When they came to the area displaying her
favorite items, he happened to be standing behind her and slid his hands around her stomach, drawing her back against him. He probably had no idea how erotic it felt to her, but
she almost fainted from the sensation and
slumped against him because her legs could
scarcely support her weight.

"Shall I tell the man to ship all of it?"

His husky voice reduced her to a throbbing
lump.

"D-do you like the set as much as I do?"
She finally managed to get the words out.

Against the side of her neck where she'd
sprayed a fresh lemon scent he murmured, "It
was my choice years ago."

The ache in his voice gave her a deeper
glimpse into his psyche and the pain he'd suffered because of his supposed inability to give
them a baby. Not all men or women cared the
same way about children, but she realized that

this moment was as earthshaking to Cord as it was to her. Whatever the future held, he would never take his fatherhood for granted. As for his being a wonderful parent, Ashley could guarantee it.

She would have liked to stay in his arms, but some other people had come to look at the furniture. Cord, too, seemed reluctant for the moment to end. "Next week we'll buy the rest of the things we need," he announced sotto voce, grasping her hand and drawing her toward the nearest counter where a salesclerk awaited them.

While he took care of their transaction and gave the address for the delivery, Cord refused to break physical contact with her. It was almost as if he was afraid she would disappear if he let her go.

True to his word, they stopped for a hamburger on the way back to the hospital. They talked about their child, what kind of parents they wanted to be. Their discussion covered the various philosophies of child-rearing and they ended up agreeing on everything.

Ashley felt a new contentment she'd never known before. But it was a little like moving through twilight slumber, not quite awake, not quite asleep, that magical time when the whole world was enveloped in a rosy glow.

Enjoy it now, her heart warned her. Life will be quite different after you leave the safety of the hospital and return to the scene of the crime.

Those were Vince's words and they haunted her. But the appellation was appropriate. A crime had been committed.

As Sister Bernice had admonished, Ashley owed it to Cord, their marriage, their baby, to find out the truth once and for all. The nun had given Ashley a lot to think about.

When she looked back on her life at the orphanage, the only truly ugly period that came to mind were the years when Marsha had tormented her. In fact it had been so bad, Ashley had blocked the memory from her mind, not recalling it until Sister Bernice had unearthed it.

Before the advent of Marsha, Ashley hadn't ever known any devious people, had never been around such a troubled person. With hindsight she could see how the older girl had manipulated every conceivable situation to hurt Ashley.

Worse, Ashley had been so naive she'd completely underestimated Marsha's ability to make real trouble, never dreaming anyone could be that disturbed. It appeared Ashley had made the same mistake with Sheila.

Cord had sworn that his stepmother had fabricated everything. If so, then Ashley—already plagued by doubts because Cord had seemed so remote since their move back to Salt Lake—had played right into Sheila's hands by running away eight months ago.

That had been Ashley's pattern at the orphanage, to flee from the pain, to hide from Marsha so that something awful wouldn't happen again.

''Ashley? We're back.''

She blinked, surprised to discover they'd pulled into a stall of the hospital parking terrace.

''What are you thinking about that has put such a fierce expression on your face?'' He'd asked the question half-mockingly, but she sensed some anxiety, as well.

"I—I guess I'm a little nervous about being a good mother," she prevaricated, though in truth she was as worried as any expectant woman about her ability to measure up to the awesome responsibility.

Like always, his quick smile turned her heart over. "You were born for the job. Of that I have no doubts." So saying, he brushed his lips against hers before levering himself from the car to come around and help her.

Whenever, wherever he touched her, he ignited new fires. It was a good thing the next few days were going to be lived in a controlled environment. With other people about—the hospital staff coming in and out of their room—they wouldn't be truly alone.

She feared that day, feared making love with him again.

Once back in his bed, in his arms, Ashley would be lost in rapture, vulnerable, open to new hurts.

She couldn't go through that again. She *refused.*

Returning home with Cord would be the ultimate experiment to see if their marriage could really work. It would test her mental and emotional fortitude in ways she didn't even want to think about.

Cord wouldn't like it, but the issue of Sheila had to be put to rest one way or the other before Ashley could once more consider becoming his wife in the Biblical sense of the word.

Before they left the hospital on Sunday, she would need to make that very clear to him. Otherwise she would have to go her own way, *alone*.

"Hey you two," Jerry called out as he passed them in the hall. "Where have you guys been?"

Cord slowed down to talk to him. "At the doctor's."

Jerry squinted. "Is everything all right?"

"More than all right," Cord answered with a satisfied sigh. "We've just found out we're going to have a boy."

"Now that's what I like to hear. Wait till I tell my wife! Tonight we'll have to have a party."

"Sounds good to us, doesn't it, darling?"

Oh, Cord. You're acting and sounding too happy. I'm afraid.

Deep in her tortured thoughts, she was scarcely aware of the rest of their walk. It wasn't until they passed the nursing station that she realized someone was talking to them.

"Mr. McKnight?"

Cord paused midstride, his hand still around Ashley's waist keeping her close to him. "Yes?"

"You have a visitor. She's in the outpatient waiting room downstairs."

CHAPTER SEVEN

ASHLEY froze in place.

Only three days' absence and already Sheila is trying to make contact. Okay. This is it. Your first test. If you can't handle it, then there's no point to anything.

"They told her that no one is allowed up here during the clinic, but she insisted it was an emergency and said she must talk to you in person."

Cord's head jerked around, his eyes darkening to a glacial midnight blue as he stared at Ashley. "I know what you're thinking," he rapped out before she could say anything. "But I swear I have no idea how she traced me here." His voice grated. "Dan's the only one at the office privy to that information. As for the rest of the staff, they're assuming I'm on a week's vacation."

"I believe you," she assured him. "Otherwise why bother to go through with the elab-

174

orate farce of getting me to attend this clinic with you.''

Cord gauged the sincerity of her words, then grasped her hand. ''As far as I'm concerned, she can go to hell. Let's get back to our room.'' His jaw had hardened so ferociously, she barely recognized him.

''No, Cord.'' She stood her ground. ''Maybe she's using this as an excuse to see you. Then again, it's possible she has news you need to hear.''

Obviously shocked by her reaction, his relentless gaze searched hers. He didn't quite trust this new side of her. She couldn't blame him. The old Ashley would have stolen quietly away, her face eloquent with anguish. Another hurt to nurse. Another wall to keep them apart.

''You don't believe that. Neither do I,'' he scathed.

Ashley stood her ground. ''Nevertheless, as long as she's here, you'd better see her.''

You may be surprised that she found out about the clinic, Cord, but you're not really surprised that she would go to these lengths to see you. You're only pretending to be because of me and the precariousness of our situation.

That had always been their problem since living in Salt Lake. Because of Sheila, they'd tried to protect each other from getting hurt. They'd bent over backward to avoid causing pain, but in the process, their efforts had only made everything worse.

She heard his harsh intake of breath. "The only way I would agree to see Sheila is with you at my side. But if it means upsetting you and the baby, I'm not prepared to take that risk."

Those words went a long way to assuage Ashley's fears. It was his method of demonstrating new resolve on his part to dispel any suspicion. Because he was trying so hard, it prompted her to say, "When you think about it, what difference does it make whether we talk to her now, or four days from now?"

There was no response. His powerful body didn't move an inch. Only his eyes spoke to her. They were asking the question he hadn't voiced. Both she and Cord were painfully aware of their tenuous new beginning. Neither one wanted to make a wrong move. Right now he was trying to do everything right. So was she.

Did she trust him? If so, she needed to proceed the way she intended to go or she'd never be whole again. What was it Sister Bernice had said? "You have a duty to your husband to put your old fears to rest once and for all."

"Let's go down right now and find out what she wants."

By the deafening silence, she realized that once again she'd surprised him. The Ashley he knew would never have suggested such a plan, let alone had the courage to carry it through.

"Please, Cord—you want me to trust you, so why not deal with her together and present a united front."

She could sense the battle going on inside him. "You're sure?" Anxiety, fear, admiration—all those emotions and more she read in his eyes.

"Actually I think I'm glad she came. If I have to see her again for the first time in months, I would just as soon it be here at the hospital with you at my side. I mean, what can she say or do in front of us that she hasn't already tried?"

His chest heaved. "If you really want to do this, then promise me you'll follow my lead.

Whatever she thinks she has to say can be accomplished in sixty seconds or less.''

Since Ashley had no desire to be in Sheila's company any longer than necessary, it was an easy promise to make.

''Shall we go?''

He put his arm around her shoulders and they retraced their footsteps. At the double doors leading to the elevator he pulled her close. ''One more thing before we leave the floor,'' he whispered.

The second she lifted her head in query, his mouth descended. He gave her a long, urgent kiss. When he finally relinquished his hold of her, she was out of breath. The blood pounded in her ears. ''Now I'm ready.''

The barely controlled ardor of his embrace left her so speechless and dull-witted, she was scarcely cognizant of their trip downstairs to the outpatient lounge.

Perhaps the one thing that helped her press forward without hesitation was the knowledge that Sheila would be expecting one person to appear in the waiting room. *Cord*.

Ashley's presence, a very *pregnant* Ashley, nestled tightly against her husband, would come as a tremendous shock.

To have that kind of advantage helped Ashley hold on to her determination. Cord must have sensed her confidence because en route he kissed the side of her neck several times.

Sheila wasn't difficult to spot. Even though Cord's stepmother was sitting with a lot of people in the crowded room, it didn't surprise Ashley that her presence dominated the scene. No matter how many attractive women there might be in a given setting, Cord's stepmother drew attention.

The first time Ashley met her, the tall, willowy blonde reminded her of Veronica Lake, a sultry movie star of the 1940 classic films whose trademark was the fall of wavy hair cascading down one side of her face.

Between her long, slender legs and the alluring way she carried herself, she was the personification of femininity. For Cord's delectation, she'd taken great pains with her appearance. The stunning champagne silk dress looked new, as did the strappy high-heels and strand of matched pearls. She looked polished, sophisticated, rich and mysterious.

For a brief moment, the old feelings of inadequacy swept through Ashley. She could never hope to compete, especially in her pregnant state. But three days of therapy plus the fact that she was carrying Cord's child had gone a long way to bolstering her self-confidence.

Additional warmth spread through her body when Cord's arm slid down her back to squeeze her waist.

''Sheila? You wanted to see me? If so, I suggest we step out into the hall where we won't be overheard.''

Cord's stepmother raised her golden head from the magazine she'd been reading. The second she saw them together, a stillness crept over her and she rose to her feet with pure feminine grace, unlike Ashley whose movements were slower and more clumsy.

When they reached the empty corridor Ashley felt Sheila's cool gray gaze stray from Cord to her, assessing her with one sweep of her long lashes, not giving any of her thoughts away. *Marsha had possessed that same unnerving ability.*

Ashley knew the other woman couldn't believe her eyes. It was a singularly triumphant moment for Ashley, yet she had to give Sheila full marks for covering up her shock so totally. Her *sangfroid* was amazing, if not daunting. Like Marsha, Sheila was a past master at mind games and manipulation, making her a dangerous adversary.

You're grown-up now, Ashley. More than equal to the task. You don't need to be afraid of Sheila anymore.

"Well, you two. This is a surprise."

Cord's arm tightened around Ashley. "That's what happens when you show up uninvited. However, the only question of significance is what you did to get Dan to reveal my whereabouts."

His words would have withered Ashley on the spot, but Sheila was a different animal and appeared unfazed by the retort.

"He called a special meeting today to tender his resignation. He gave no explanation, then he walked out."

Ashley felt Cord's body harden. Dan Locke had been with the company forty-plus years, serving in every capacity until he'd worked his way up to vice president in charge of operations. This had to come as a tremendous blow to Cord.

"He wouldn't have done that unless he was provoked beyond reason," her husband's voice rasped.

"I knew this would be upsetting to you. In an effort to get him to reconsider, I called his wife. She refused to tell me anything. She said you were the only person she would talk to, but that you were participating in the Great Salt Lake Smokeout Clinic and were unavailable."

Ashley couldn't help but wonder what unscrupulous tactics Sheila had used to get Dan's sweet wife to reveal Cord's whereabouts. It must have been a devastating moment for Emily Locke.

"Since by fair means or foul you found out where I was, it was your duty as an officer in the company to have phoned me immediately and left that message with the clerk at the nursing station," Cord bit out, visibly upset by the news of Dan. "For several reasons, your coming to the hospital was unconscionable." He continued to chastise her without scruple. "Let's go, Ashley." He raised his arm to her shoulders.

"There's something else," Sheila added without a qualm.

Ashley knew it.

Cord hugged her tighter. "Nothing could be more important than the tragic news about the best man in the entire company. As you can see, my wife is expecting our son very soon and it's past our bedtime."

"*Your* son, Cord?"

For once Sheila couldn't hide her shock. It shouldn't have delighted Ashley so much.

"That's right. A man should be so lucky as to experience one miracle in his lifetime. This week I've been afforded two." As he said the words, he turned his head to gaze down at Ashley. "My wife has come back to me and my cup runneth over," he murmured before kissing her full on the mouth in front of Sheila.

Ashley's heart streamed into his, blotting out the ache and the hurt. She gave herself up fully to his kiss, permeated by a joy she didn't know how she was going to contain.

"I couldn't be happier with your news. When can I expect you two home?"

With a reluctance Ashley could sense, Cord finally lifted his head. "Sunday night," he murmured thickly before ushering them both from the lounge.

The fact that Cord didn't mention Dan's name until they'd reached their room upstairs testified to the measure of entrancement that held them both.

For Ashley, something magical had happened downstairs just now. The weight of distrust and suspicion seemed to have evaporated the moment Cord proclaimed his happiness in front of Sheila.

"Darling?" He grasped her hands and kissed them. "All I want to do is concentrate on you, on us, but—"

"I know—" she broke in, standing on tiptoe to brush his lips. "Dan needs you. While you talk to him, I'll go watch a movie with the others."

His hands tightened in her hair, his eyes blazing with a new light. "I'll join you as soon as I can," he promised, giving her another drugging kiss that left them both trembling before she left the room.

The film was halfway over when Cord eventually found his seat next to Ashley at the back of the auditorium. Reaching for her hand, he gripped it tightly.

"Did you get hold of him?" she whispered.

"Yes."

Alarmed by his clipped tone, she looked at him in the near darkness. "It's bad, isn't it?"

Cord stared at her. "Yes. He doesn't want to talk about it."

"Not even to *you*?" She frowned.

He shook his head. "That's what is so puzzling."

Sheila had something to do with it, but Ashley didn't want to be the one to bring his stepmother's name into the conversation, not tonight of all nights.

Ashley and Cord had just reached a new understanding. She couldn't bear for anything to rob them of the pleasure of this special time together. Too soon they'd be back at the house, their privacy almost nonexistent with Sheila living there.

"Didn't he say *anything* to help you understand his motives?"

"Only that he feels it's time to move on."

"But that's absurd!" Ashley cried softly. "He's too valuable to lose and too old to start a new career."

"I couldn't agree with you more. Something bizarre has happened or he wouldn't just quit. I asked him to meet me tomorrow, but he refused and said he'd have his desk cleaned out first thing in the morning."

Ashley clutched his hand harder. This was a new contingency neither of them had counted on. "Then you're going to have to do something about it tonight."

She felt him stiffen. "I'm not leaving you," he said like an avowal.

"You won't have to if we go over to his house together."

"No, Ashley," he muttered emphatically. "It's late. You need your rest. I don't want you dragged into this, especially not this close to your due date."

"I'm not a fragile piece of glass, Cord. Whatever my origins, I must have come from sturdy stock because I feel fine, and I can handle this. What affects you, affects me."

"*Lord*— It's been too long since I heard you say that to me. Do you have any idea how much I love you?" His voice throbbed with a new intensity of emotion. "I wanted tonight to be special for us."

She thrilled to those words. *So did I, darling. So did I.*

Kissing the back of his hand, she whispered, "We have the rest of our lives to talk and show each other how we feel. But there's something we have to do first. Emily must be in agony. She trusts you. In fact I know she thinks the world of you, Cord. I have an idea we can work on him through her."

"If anyone can get to her, *you* can, my love. She took to you the first time she met you at the company picnic."

Cord spoke the truth. She and Emily connected from day one. "Then let's not waste another second. While you get permission for us to leave the hospital, I'll go back to the room and freshen up."

"You're sure you want to do this?"

She was touched by his concern, but this was one time when someone else's needs came first.

"Cord? Forget me. Please. Time is of the essence here. If Dan is really upset, he might be planning to leave town after he clears out his desk. You know he's the quiet type who suffers instead of getting things out in the open. It would be just like him to disappear somewhere to lick his wounds, whatever they are. You can't let that happen without a fight."

In the obscure light his eyes kindled with new fire. "You're right. You're also astute, which is one of the many things I admire and love about you."

"And you're a caring man," she returned the compliment. "It's one of your sterling qualities. But be honest, darling. If it weren't for me, you'd be over at Dan's house right now."

In a surprise move, Cord rose from the seat and half pulled her up with him. His reaction sent the adrenaline surging through her nervous system. As soon as they'd cleared the auditorium doors, he forced her around to face him. His dark brows had furrowed ominously.

"Let's get something straight," he began, his hands forming fists at his sides. She could sense the struggle he was having to tamp down his feelings. "You and the baby are my first priority. Now, and forever. Is that clear?"

"Yes," she whispered, loving him more than ever before. But by his slight hesitation she could tell he was still afraid to believe the drastic change in her feelings.

Small wonder. After all the months of trauma they'd lived through, their reconciliation was another miracle.

"Why don't you see about getting permission for us to leave?"

Heaving a deep sigh, he kissed the end of her nose. "I'll be back before you know it."

They took their leave of each other and she hurried down the hall for a quick shower and change of clothes. After the ultrasound, she wanted to wash off any residue gel and feel fresh.

When she emerged, she was wearing the smart navy blue and green plaid jumper with a navy silk blouse she'd bought. The tailored outfit was comfortable and suited her pregnant figure.

"You look very attractive, Mrs. McKnight," Cord commented seconds later when she announced herself ready to go. Heat traveled through her body as his eyes played over her, the look of desire unmistakable.

"Thank you." She swallowed hard. "So do you."

While she'd been in the shower, he'd come back to the room and had changed into a dark, olive-green suit. "That's my favorite outfit on you, Cord."

"It has always been mine, too, because you picked it out for me."

Both of them were remembering the morning she'd pulled the new suit out of the closet she'd bought for him with her own savings.

With his wealth he could buy most anything, but her gift was something she'd wanted to do for him. Her surprise had pleased him so much, he'd taken the day off and they'd ended up making love for most of it.

"We match," she blurted in an effort to clear her mind of pictures too thrilling and intimate to entertain right now.

"In all the ways that count," came the thick-toned rejoinder. "Are you ready to go?"

"Yes."

After they'd left the hospital and were driving out of the parking lot, Ashley turned to him. "What did Dr. Drake say about our leaving?"

"He realizes that emergencies crop up. As long as you're with me, he feels fine about it. No doubt our esteemed psychologist has been giving him updates. Secretly I believe both of them are so pleased that you and I have reconciled, the renowned Dr. Drake is willing to waive the usual rules for us."

Her face grew warm. "I'm sure you're right. So far I haven't noticed the other couples being given any special favors." Just thinking of their newly-made friends reminded her of the reason why they had come to the hospital in the first place. "Cord? Have these four days without a cigarette been hard for you?"

"Yes," he said emotively. "But not in the way you mean. Since I first saw you on Monday morning, I've only suffered from one craving."

She lowered her head, so sick with excitement and wanting, she couldn't say anything.

"I've missed sleeping with you," he murmured. "You *know* how it always was with us." His low, vibrant voice penetrated to her insides.

"I remember." Her whisper came out more like an ache. "I—I've been in agony, too."

His hand slid to her thigh, caressing it with urgency. "When I think of my beautiful wife alone and pregnant all this time... The nights of loving we've missed..."

She put a trembling hand over his. "Let's not look back. No more regrets."

"If we didn't have unfinished business, I'd keep on driving until we reached our cabin in the Tetons."

"I couldn't imagine anything more wonderful."

"Ashley—" His voice had dropped to a lower register. "Art Williams phoned me last month. He's been offered the job of head ranger in Yellowstone and wanted me to know about it before it was posted. Though there's a long list of applicants for the vacancy he'll be leaving, apparently he has already recommended me to replace him as head ranger in the Tetons."

"*Cord*!" Ashley's ecstatic cry filled the Rover's interior.

A satisfied smile broke the corner of his sensuous mouth. "I thought maybe that news would appeal to you. It's what I've always wanted." His voice throbbed. "But because we were separated, I couldn't imagine taking on the job without you."

Oh, Cord— "I—I had no idea."

"His cabin is larger than the one we lived in. We'd have plenty of room to raise our son."

"Do it!" she urged him. "Call Art and tell him you want the job!"

"I will, just as soon as we've talked to Dan. He deserves to be the CEO of the company. When I tell him that the whole board will be behind him if I step down, that ought to open him up so he'll tell me what's wrong. No doubt Sheila is at the crux of his troubles," he said in a menacing tone.

Ashley had no doubts, either, but was thankful Cord had been the one to voice them. "Can't she block a move like that because your dad left her his shares?"

''No,'' came the emphatic pronouncement. ''I inherited mother's shares, something my father couldn't touch. If I exercise my right and vote like the others, Sheila will find herself without a position in the company, though she'll always receive an income from the profits.

''When she discovers that you and I are going to live in the Tetons and she's virtually alone, we can always hope she'll disappear from the state.''

''I don't think she'll give up the house,'' Ashley murmured.

''Maybe not. But as soon as our baby is born, we'll never live there again so it doesn't matter. My life is with you and our son.''

''That was your home, Cord!''

''*Was* being the operative word. The day my father let her inside, my life changed forever. She can do whatever she wants with it after we leave. You and I are going to create our own memories elsewhere, so let's not talk about it again.''

They'd been holding such an intense conversation, Ashley hadn't realized that they'd already arrived at Dan's Colonial-style house in North Salt Lake.

Cord turned off the ignition and came around to her side of the Land Rover to help her down. She could see lights on in the front windows. "Both their cars are still in the carport, Cord. That's a good sign."

He unexpectedly lowered his mouth to hers in a long, satisfying kiss. "Having you here with me like this makes all the difference, Ashley. Let's go."

As they headed toward the porch, Ashley realized that Cord wasn't the same man who four days ago had passed her by in the hospital corridor looking ill and haunted.

The attractive, hard-muscled male who escorted her up the steps with a possessive arm, walked with new purpose. The combination of their reconciliation and impending fatherhood had given him a whole new reason to be alive. That elation was infectious and had spilled over to her, making her believe that the nightmare they'd lived through was almost behind them.

Almost.

If they found out Cord's stepmother had something to do with Dan's resignation, then Ashley would feel more empowered than ever to help expose Sheila for the liar she was. Hopefully Cord would be able to convince Dan to stay with the company and see this dark period through to a satisfactory conclusion.

"*Cord*! *Ashley*?" Dan's wife said in surprise when she saw them standing on the other side of the screen. Her eyes darted back and forth between them. "But I thought—"

"We know what you thought," Cord finished the sentence for her. "Ashley and I are back together. As you can see, we're expecting a baby."

Emily's eyes widened. "But—"

"It's a long story, Emily. Right now we've come as friends to talk to you and Dan. Would that be all right?"

"Yes. Of course." She opened the screen so they could enter. "Dan's up in the bedroom. Maybe I can get him to co—"

"Who's at the door, Em?" Dan called out.

"It's Cord and Ashley!"

After a long silence, "Just a minute."

Emily sighed her relief and told them to follow her into the living room where Cord drew Ashley over to the velvet couch and pulled her down next to him. As soon as they were seated, Dan appeared in the entry dressed in casual trousers and a plaid shirt.

Ashley had never seen him in anything but a conservative suit and tie. Ironically, the warm, affable personality she associated with him was missing. In its place he presented a guarded, reserved demeanor totally uncharacteristic of him.

He stared at Ashley in stunned surprise. "What's going on here?"

Cord smiled, hugging her close. "My wife and I are back together, and we're expecting a son in about three weeks."

Dan's skin held a distinct pallor. "It's *your* baby?"

Ashley couldn't prevent the gasp that escaped. "Who else's would it be?"

"I'm sorry," Dan muttered. "I didn't mean to upset you, Ashley. Everybody knew you and Cord hadn't been able to have children, and then there was talk that you and—" He stopped midsentence. "Forget it. Obviously it wasn't true."

"You mean that rumor Sheila spread about me and Greg Ferris?"

She noticed a shadow in Cord's eyes before her glance flicked to Dan who had the grace to look sheepish. "I don't remember. Maybe."

"Besides Cord and me, she's done Greg and Bonnie a terrible injustice. Especially when he was the one instrumental in getting Cord and me back together. For the record, I conceived our baby right before Cord and I separated. The doctor said we made medical history."

"That's wonderful!" Emily ejaculated, clearly thrilled by the news. It warmed Ashley's heart, but she could tell Cord was upset.

He rose to his imposing height. "We were hoping you would be happy for us, Dan, but that isn't the reason we're here." With his powerful legs slightly apart he said, "We've been friends too many years for our association to end like this. How come it took Sheila to tell me that you had resigned? If there were serious problems, why didn't you unload to me before I checked into the hospital?"

Ashley noticed that he couldn't look Cord in the eye. Something was terribly wrong.

"I thought it would be better this way."

Cord shook his head. "Not better for the company surely. The fact is, before too much longer, the board will be voting you in as the new CEO."

Dan looked up at him, dazed. "Sheila's never going to let that happen."

His dark brows quirked. "Obviously you know something that I don't."

Ashley could tell that Dan was squirming inwardly. "Cord—" he began, then hesitated, but there was a wealth of pain mixed with anguish in that one word.

"You don't have to tell me anything if you don't want to. It can keep. But I'm letting you know... Sheila is on her way out and she doesn't have a choice."

Dan grimaced. "The only way that could happen is if *you* voted against her."

"That's right."

Now it was Dan's turn to stand up. "But I don't understand. I thought—" He paused again and scratched his head. "Your dad—"

"I don't want to talk about my father," Cord interrupted, his mouth twisting unpleasantly. "You know the old saying. You can't choose your relatives. Sheila's never been good for the company."

At this point Ashley got up from the couch and put her arm through Cord's. "She has hurt a lot of people in the past, including Cord's mother. She's still trying to come between Cord and me. We're not going to let it happen again."

For that show of loyalty, Cord bestowed a kiss on her temple. "It's time we all closed ranks on Sheila, Dan. It's going to take a little planning and strategy, but we can do it.

"Why don't you stay out of the office until the end of the week? On Monday we'll both show up for work as usual. When she asks you what you're doing there, you can tell her the truth. That you changed your mind. That's all she needs to know.

"We'll proceed as normal until it's time to give her her walking papers. Think about it and phone me before the weekend is over. Right now my wife is swaying on her feet. I need to get her to bed."

Cord spoke the truth. Since Sheila's visit, Ashley had been on an emotional roller coaster and was truly exhausted.

The older couple walked them to the door. "I'll call you," Dan agreed at last.

"Bless you for coming over tonight," Emily added. "As for you, Ashley, Cord's right. You're about ready to topple."

"I'll take care of her."

Cord's silky avowal reminded her that they were really back together again. It was wonderful. She needed to tell him all the things she was feeling in her heart, but too much had happened in one day. It was impossible to stay awake and she eventually fell into a deep sleep on the way back to the hospital.

Aside from a feeling of being cherished, she remembered nothing of the walk to their floor or being put to bed.

CHAPTER EIGHT

"*CORD*—" she murmured groggily. "What time is it?"

"Ten to eight."

"You're kidding! I thought it must be the middle of the night!"

She bolted straight up in bed but had forgotten her stomach was in the way. Once again her muscles protested and she let out a muffled groan.

In an instant he reached her side, molding his palm to her sleep-warmed cheek. "What's wrong?" He sounded so anxious, she sat there in amazement.

"N-nothing," she stammered. The loose green robe revealed his hair-dusted chest, reminding her that he was wearing nothing else underneath. His hands anywhere on her body created overwhelming excitement. "I just sat up too fast. These days I need to move v-e-r-y carefully."

His hard-boned physique relaxed, but his hands had slid down her arms. ''You're telling me the truth?'' he demanded with a gentle shake.

In the obscure light, it was impossible to see the deep blue of his eyes, but she could feel his glance wandering over her. The covers had fallen around her hips, exposing her swollen belly to his probing gaze.

''I promise,'' she said in a tiny voice.

''Swear you'll never lie to me about your condition.''

''I swear it.''

''I'll need more proof,'' he came back gruffly.

Before she could think, his head descended, blotting out all light. He'd trapped her mouth with his own.

The force of his passion drove her back against the pillow. Ashley let out a slight gasp before she found herself being hungrily devoured.

Caught completely off guard, she began returning her husband's ardor with a ferocity that knew no bounds. Without realizing it, her hands crept up his chest to clasp him around the neck. Their kiss deepened. She never wanted it to end.

Somehow, she didn't know how, Cord had stretched out on the hospital bed beside her, the fingers of one hand twisted in her short hair as he covered her face and neck with kisses.

"*Darling*," he whispered against her lips, kissing them over and over again. "Last night you fell asleep on me, and now I want you so much I'm burning alive. You want me, too. I can tell because wherever I touch you, you tremble," he murmured provocatively against her throat where a little pulse raced. "Sit up a little so I can remove your—"

"Good morning you two."

"*Vince*—" they both cried at the same time.

Turning every shade of red, Ashley pulled the sheet over her head.

"Sorry to disturb. It looks like you two forgot about breakfast. I'll come back in five minutes. All right?"

"I guess it will have to be," Cord mocked dryly. She felt the mattress give as he got to his feet. "But I'm letting you know right now your timing is lousy."

Ashley heard Vince's delighted chuckle before he left them alone again.

"While you turn yourself into a decent woman, Mrs. McKnight, I'll put on some clothes and bring us back whatever's left of breakfast."

Anything she might have said in response was smothered by another hungry kiss before he helped her from the bed.

"Oh, boy," she muttered in self-disgust as she fairly waddled across the room.

Cord's teasing laughter didn't help as she closed the bathroom door on him. She never expected to hear that happy sound again and leaned against it for a minute. This morning, her joy could hardly be contained.

Fortunately for her and Cord, Vince gave them closer to a half hour before he returned to the room. In that amount of time they'd eaten, and Ashley had made herself presentable in one of her pants and flowered tops.

Every time she looked at Cord's virile, good looks, dressed for comfort in well-worn jeans and T-shirt, her heart turned over.

When all three were seated, Vince glanced from one to the other, his gaze speculative. "Was it only Monday morning that the two caring, intelligent people in this room couldn't talk to each other because they were in so much pain?

"Now it's Friday, and lo and behold, not only do I discover that you're both still here— I find I need to make appointments with you so I won't walk in on the late late show."

Ashley laughed quietly while Cord sat there grinning.

"I take it this time at the clinic has done wonders for your marriage."

Cord grasped Ashley's hand and held on to it. "It has, Vince."

"Thank you for putting up with us," Ashley chimed in.

"I couldn't be happier. Naturally I'm hoping that because you've resolved some major problems, your desire to smoke will diminish and you'll use the tools you've learned here to combat the urge when it does crop up."

"To be honest, Vince, while we've been in here, I haven't even thought about it."

"That's good. But remember that this has been a safe place. There will come a time after you've left the hospital when you'll be vulnerable again."

Cord's dark blue gaze sobered as it flicked to Ashley and lingered. "We both realize that."

We do. We still have Sheila to face.

"All right. Now, for some information which we need to discuss. The hospital has planned a surprise weekend outing down to Bryce and Zion Canyons. It was announced at breakfast but you weren't there."

Ashley blinked in surprise.

"We'll be leaving in the vans within a half hour. It's important that Cord goes. There will be group therapy sessions during this period which are a vital part of the program.

"But at this late stage in your pregnancy, Ashley, the discomfort of riding long distances, plus the walking and horseback riding make it prohibitive for you to go. In fact, Dr. Drake won't allow it because he wouldn't want you to be that far away from your doctor in case of an emergency. There would be legal ramifications, as you can imagine.

"Therefore you'll have to remain behind while I ride with Cord. Just remember that you're free to stay here at the hospital until our return Sunday afternoon for a final meeting. But if that doesn't appeal, you're welcome to go home, whatever you prefer."

"She'll stay *here*," Cord made the split-second decision in no uncertain terms.

"Good." Vince got up from the chair. "Then I won't keep you two any longer since you've got some packing to do. Meet me in the lounge in twenty minutes, all right, Cord?"

Ashley shouldn't have been so upset by the announcement that her husband was going to have to leave her for a couple of days. The whole reason he had come into the hospital was to take advantage of the therapy offered.

When she thought about it, an outing in nature sounded like a wonderful idea, something all the people involved in the program needed at this point so the walls wouldn't close in on them.

But she and Cord had just gotten back to-gether and the idea of another separation, no matter how short—

"I'm in as much pain as you are," Cord whispered, coming up from behind to slide his arms around her. "*Lord*—leaving you is the last thing I want to do right now. I had no idea a trip was part of the program."

"Neither did I, but it will be good for you. As for me, I'll do a little shopping for the baby and finish the quilt."

"Don't go out, Ashley. We'll shop next week. Just stay here where I know you're safe. I don't want you taking any chances. Promise that you'll mind me this one time."

She heard his fear and knew he worried about her condition. *About Sheila.*

Ashley's eyes closed tightly. "I promise."

The next few minutes passed by in a blur while Cord showered and dressed. Ashley au-tomatically helped him pack what he would need, but the silence between them was testi-mony of a new tension brought on by the knowledge that they were going to be sepa-rated again.

Once he'd shut his case, his probing gaze studied her closed expression. "I can't do it, Ashley." He shook his dark head. "I can't leave you."

She realized it was up to her if he went or not. When she'd run away from him almost eight months ago, it had done even more damage than she'd realized. To *both* of them.

"You *have* to go." On a burst of pure inspiration she ventured, "Would you feel better if I went to the orphanage and stayed there until you came for me? I always have a place with Sister Bernice. She'll guard me with a vengeance."

Actually when she thought about it, being around the wise nun was exactly what Ashley needed right now.

Though he didn't immediately say anything, something flickered in the recesses of his eyes, giving her his answer. He wanted her safe, out of harm's way. Out of Sheila's way... He trusted Sister Bernice.

"Only if I thought you wouldn't do any work."

She smiled. "Taking care of the babies is a joy. Besides, it wouldn't hurt me to have one last refresher course before my permanent job begins. If you have the opportunity to be near a phone during the trip, all you have to do is call the orphanage.''

''You would do that for me?'' Though his breath sounded ragged, she could hear his relief.

''I think my presence here this week should convince you that I'd do anything to make our marriage work.''

In the next instant she was crushed in his arms, baby and all. ''So would I, Ashley. *Anything.*''

His mouth descended on hers in a fiery kiss that burned its way through to her soul. ''I love you, darling,'' he whispered before finally lifting his head.

Her blue eyes stared longingly into his. ''I love you, too, Cord. From the very first moment you appeared on that mountain ledge, my life has never been the same. If our awful separation has taught me one thing, it's that my world makes no sense without you.''

''*Amen,*'' he muttered fiercely. After one more soul-destroying kiss, he helped pack her things. As they passed the nursing station, he informed the person in charge of their plans. With another aside to Vince who said the vans were parked at the west entrance, she and Cord left the floor together.

Not satisfied until she was in her car and had backed out, he stood watching with that proprietorial look she loved, hands on his hips. "Expect me sometime Sunday afternoon."

She leaned out the window for one last kiss. "You stay safe, too," she ordered before driving off, her eyes misty. "I—I couldn't handle it if anything happened to you."

His face darkened with lines. "Nothing's going to happen. Not to either of us. We have a son to raise and the rest of our lives to love each other. Just hold that thought."

"I will."

The hardest thing Ashley ever had to do was drive away from him. Thank heaven she *was* going to St. Anne's.

When she reached the orphanage twenty minutes later, it appeared she'd walked in on a minor crisis because several of the help were down with the flu. Ashley could see another pair of hands were needed.

Sister Bernice appeared thrilled to see her and told her she was welcome to stay. But when Ashley offered to help out, the nun refused, reminding Ashley she needed to take care of herself this close to her delivery date.

Naturally Ashley recognized that there were a lot of jobs she shouldn't do. But she knew the orphanage routine blindfolded, and after depositing her things in one of the rooms designated for new arrivals, she went to the nursery. Sister Bernice wouldn't get too upset if Ashley helped feed a couple of the babies.

Though thoughts of her husband never left her mind, Ashley found that being with the babies made the hours fly by. When she went to bed that night, she was asleep before her head even touched the pillow.

Saturday she slept in, but by afternoon, she reported to the nursery again. She hadn't been there long before she was called to Sister Bernice's office.

''There's a call for you,'' the nun said with a decided twinkle in her eye before she left the room to give Ashley her privacy.

She thanked her, then picked up the receiver with trembling hands. ''*Cord*?''

"Darling?"

Ashley sank down on the chair. "I—I'm so glad you called."

"Then you have some idea of how I'm feeling right now," came his impassioned murmur. "This was my first opportunity. Sister Bernice told me you've been helping in the nursery. She also said you were an angel sent straight from heaven, but I could have told her that already."

Too overcome with emotion she could only murmur, "It's therapy." After swallowing hard, "How are you? How is it going?"

"It's good. I'm learning a lot. Being down here makes me hunger for the life we're going to have in the Tetons. I've got plans, Ashley. I can't wait to talk to you about them when I get home tomorrow."

She gripped the phone tighter. "Do you know when that will be?"

"Around five in the afternoon. Vince has taken pity on me and says I don't have to stay for the last meeting at the hospital. I'm free to come for you."

She sucked in her breath. "I can't wait."

"Neither can I. Two nights away from you
are killing me. After tomorrow we're never going to be parted again."

"No. *Never.*"

"*Ashley*—" He started to say something,
then she heard voices. "Darling? It looks like
I have to get off. Someone else needs to use
the phone."

To have to hang up now came as a crushing
blow. She fought to stay composed, but her
voice cracked when she said, "I understand.
Goodnight, my love."

"See you in my dreams."

The phone went dead.

Sister Bernice had just said goodnight to one
of the children and was returning to her office
when she saw Ashley. "Is everything all right
with your husband?"

Ashley nodded.

"Good." The older nun smiled. "But I
sense the next twelve hours or so are going to
be hard to get through without him."

At that comment, Ashley blushed. "I'm
transparent. I know."

"It's wonderful to see you so happy. I want
you to stay that way when you go home with

him tomorrow. No matter what problems you have to face, always remember how you're feeling tonight—and you'll get through them.''

She nodded. "I plan to take your advice.''

"Good. Now let's talk about tomorrow. I have an expectant mother coming to see me in the morning. She's thinking of giving up her baby.''

A subject Ashley understood only too well. Her own biological mother obviously couldn't have given Ashley a good life and did the right thing by bringing her to the orphanage.

"She'll be here at the time I normally conduct the singing and stories for the Sunday school.''

"I'll be glad to do it for you,'' Ashley said without having to be asked. Sunday school was a favorite time for the children and staff, and it was the kind of job she could handle at this late stage in her pregnancy.

"Bless you. I'm afraid you'll have to handle everything by yourself. Sister Clarisse is still sick and won't be able to accompany you on the piano.''

"That's all right. We'll get along fine.''

Before Ashley went to bed, she set things up in the room where she herself had attended hundreds of religious instruction classes. After mentally working out a program for the next morning, she went to bed exhausted but excited because tomorrow afternoon Cord would be coming for her.

Sunday turned out to be a warm, beautiful day. Ashley woke up feeling euphoric and set about her tasks with joy.

Following procedure, as soon as the closing song and prayer had been given, the children were excused from class to go outside on the enclosed grounds and play until lunch.

Satisfied that everything had gone well, Ashley put all the pictures and charts back in the cupboard and then headed for the kitchen to grab a bite of lunch.

But an all too familiar figure in a stunning lime green dress had just come out of Sister Bernice's office. Ashley's heart dropped to her feet, and she came to an abrupt standstill.

Sheila.

For the moment they were alone. Obviously she had either phoned or gone by the hospital to see Cord. When she had discovered that he was unavailable, she'd somehow managed to wangle Ashley's whereabouts from the clerk on the floor.

It would be dangerous to ever underestimate Cord's stepmother who allowed nothing to get in her way when she wanted something. *Or someone.*

Cord would be furious, but no more so than Ashley.

Dispensing with civility she demanded, "What are you doing here, Sheila? What is so important that you couldn't have waited until Cord and I arrived home tonight?"

The other woman's eyes silently mocked her. "You have an inflated sense of your own self-importance, Ashley. As it happens, I didn't come to see you and had no idea you were here. But I should have guessed. After all, this *is* where you belong."

"That's correct. St. Anne's is my home away from home. I have the legitimate right to be here."

"If you're implying that I don't, then think again. It's a state-run institution. Anyone from the streets is welcome here."

'True, Sheila. Even you...''

Ashley couldn't help turning the insult back on the other woman with the greatest of relish.

Sheila's pewter eyes darkened a trifle. "Cord never did have a clue that behind your insipid facade you're as tough as nails. It's incredible that for such an intelligent man, he wondered needlessly about how you would fend for yourself after you left him. The poor thing was on the verge of worrying himself sick over your disappearance, fearing you had no place to go, no one to take care of you."

That news was music to Ashley's ears. "Cord always was a giver. He always will be."

She thought Sheila's mouth hardened a fraction. "Nevertheless, when he couldn't find you, I urged him not to worry and reminded him that Greg was extremely fond of you. Naturally he would see to it that you didn't end up abandoned the way you once were as a child."

Ashley could sense exactly where this conversation was headed. "As Cord and I explained earlier, Greg's not the father, Sheila."

It felt good to know that for once Ashley could trust the source of her information, which was *herself*.

No doubt Sheila had planted that particular poison about Greg in Cord's mind the very first day of Ashley's disappearance. No wonder Greg's name was the first one to pass Cord's lips when he saw her last Monday morning in the advanced stages of pregnancy. It could have destroyed his friendship with the other man.

Thank heaven Greg had refused to allow that to happen. If anything, he'd risked Ashley's displeasure when he'd broken his promise to her by giving Cord her phone number.

But he'd done it for the purest of reasons. *No greater love can a man show, than he lay down his life for his friend.* Ashley loved Greg for staying loyal to both of them through such a dark period. One day she'd find a way to thank him properly.

"Whatever you came for, it will have to wait until tonight. I have work to do." She put a hand on the banister to start up the stairs, aware of Sheila's unflattering perusal.

"Those swollen fect look sore."

Another jab which should have hurt, but didn't. "Swollen feet, stretch marks, weight gain—they're all a small price to pay for bringing a child into the world. Especially a miracle child."

It was obvious Sheila didn't know what to make of this new dimension to Ashley's psyche which allowed her to stand her ground instead of retreating from the enemy.

"Miracle?" Sheila's question held the faint tinge of mockery.

Was it wrong to be enjoying this so much? "Hmm... Every child brought into this world is a miracle, don't you think?"

"Is that what the nuns taught you?"

"Of course. But I discovered the miracle for myself the other day when Cord and I saw our own baby moving inside me during the ultrasound."

Sheila's regard was vaguely speculative. "You look ready to deliver. I'm surprised you didn't stay in the hospital."

"Sorry to disappoint you, Sheila, but before that happens I'm going to be living at home with Cord another few weeks. Of course, after the baby is born, we've been discussing other plans.''

For once the other woman didn't have an immediate comeback. It allowed Ashley to luxuriate in the moment which reminded her a lot of fly-fishing with Cord.

Her husband had taught her how to cast, to throw out the line and land the fly in just the right spot. He showed her how to play with a fish, to fool it and bait it, then pop it right out of the water when the fish least expected it.

The temptation to play with Sheila the same way was overpowering. But necessity prompted her to come to the point.

''I don't know what you thought you would accomplish by showing up here. You tried your hardest to come between Cord and me, but you didn't succeed. The clinic brought us back together. As Cord told you, there's not going to be a divorce.''

Sheila's eyes filled with silent laughter. ''Oh, Ashley. You're so naive. It's incredible to me *that* ruse to get you to the hospital actually worked.''

Don't let her bait you. ''It wasn't a ruse, Sheila.''

"Oh, come on now. We both know Cord doesn't have a smoking problem. He never did. In fact he hates it. For years he has begged me to quit. Honestly, have you ever caught him lighting up? Even once? Greg mastermided that idea weeks ago."

The mention of Greg set off alarm bells. Ashley's heart started to thud. "What are you talking about?"

"Cord was very upset because you wouldn't accept any alimony. He has this idea that you couldn't exist without him because you had no family, no place to go. He felt sorry for you.

"When Greg could see Cord wasn't about to give up until he found you, he told him he knew where you living, but that you had sworn him to secrecy. He told Cord you were so bitter, you never wanted to see him again."

Ashley was trying hard not to take any of it in, but with every word uttered, she could feel a distinct chill taking over her body.

"Cord said he didn't buy that, and wanted to meet with you face to face, to see for himself that you were all right." She gave an elegant shrug of her silk-clad shoulders. "At that point Greg felt compelled to do something, so he suggested the clinic, and said he would try to get you to cooperate.''

Don't listen to her, Ashley.

"Obviously it worked," Sheila continued. "What surprises me is that you fell for that bit about his nonexistent smoking problem. But now that I think about it, you probably *didn't*. In fact I have every suspicion to believe you were glad to be rescued this close to having your baby. Of course your pride wouldn't allow you to go crawling back to Cord, not after that exit you made."

Ashley started to feel sick to her stomach.

"The clinic provided you with the excuse to cling to him and has helped you save face. As for Cord, he's now satisfied that you're not lying destitute in some dark alley on the wrong side of the tracks where most likely you were born. When you think about it, all in all it couldn't have worked out more perfectly since Cord fathered your child."

No matter that you're dying another death, don't run from this, Ashley. Don't give her the satisfaction.

"Yes. He *did*. What do you mean, it couldn't have worked out more perfectly?"

To Ashley's shock Sheila's eyes suddenly filled with tears, a sight Ashley never expected to see. "Since I know you never lie, then that truly is miraculous news."

"Don't pretend you're happy for us!" Ashley lashed out.

Sheila shook her head. "I'm not pretending. You don't understand. You see I, too, am expecting a baby."

Ashley heard Sheila's words but was in no state to comprehend them.

"There's a man I've been seeing on an occasional basis," Sheila went on talking, "but we've been taking precautions because neither of us has a desire to marry, let alone have a baby. Naturally my pregnancy came as a great shock.

"Of course if I don't want to stay pregnant, then I need to do something about it right away. It's the real reason I stopped by the hospital the other night to talk to Cord. I wanted to discuss when would be the best time to take off from business to go into the hospital to end it.

"But, Ashley—when you two told me you were pregnant with Cord's baby, I realized that meant I could be carrying Cord's baby, too. You see, all the times we've made love, we've never taken precautions because we thought he was impotent.

"In fact because the other man and I always used protection, it leads me to believe this baby probably is Cord's, a second miracle child.

"If that's the case, I intend to go full term. You don't know how hard Cord's father and I tried to have children. He wanted another son to carry on the business because he knew Cord hated it.

"I wanted to give him that son, but he was killed too soon for that to happen. Whoever dreamed I might be able to fulfill that hope through Cord.

"Imagine, Ashley—both of us pregnant with his children."

Ashley knew her body was standing there, but she felt like she had somehow escaped it and no longer had the power to make it function.

"Now that you know, would you do a favor for me?" She reached in her handbag and pulled out what looked like a business card.

"Here—" She pushed a card in her hand. "Will you see that he gets this? It's a reminder of the next appointment with my obstetrician. If Cord needs verification that I'm two months along, he's free to call him at that number any time."

On the verge of being violently ill right there on the stairs Ashley muttered, "Your story is unbelievable, Sheila. But even if you are pregnant with some man's child, if you think for one second Cord won't insist on DNA testing to ascertain paternity, then you don't know him."

"Oh— I plan to have that done the second the baby is born. If Cord's not the father of my child, then I'm going to put it up for adoption. That's the reason why I made an appointment to see Sister Bernice. I have it on your authority that she takes the best care of orphans."

Sheila was the woman Sister Bernice had been talking to?

"By the way, how soon can I expect you and Cord home? We have a lot of plans to make. It looks like we're going to have to get busy preparing *two* nurseries."

"You're *lying*, Sheila. Now get out!"

The other woman hunched her shoulders and started for the front door.

"I realize you don't believe me. But there is one way to learn the truth. Call Greg since you trust him so implicitly. He'll verify everything I've said."

CHAPTER NINE

BE HOME, *Greg.*

The phone rang several times and Bonnie answered. For the life of her, Ashley couldn't make small talk and simply asked if she could speak to Greg. In a quiet tone of voice Bonnie said she'd get him, no doubt realizing something was terribly wrong.

"Ashley, honey?" Greg got on quickly. "Are you calling from the hospital?"

"No. St. Anne's."

"What are you doing there?" he asked in an anxious voice.

"Helping out until Cord comes for me later. He's on his way home from Bryce and Zion's with the group from the clinic."

She tried to swallow to get moisture back in her mouth. "Greg—just answer me one question. It has to be the truth. It's a m-matter of life and death to me." Her whole body was shaking, not just her voice.

"What's happened?" He sounded haunted.

"The truth, Greg!"

"So help me God," came the grating rejoinder.

She filled her lungs with life-giving air. "Does Cord have a smoking problem?"

"What kind of a question is that?" Greg demanded, sounding angrier than she'd ever heard him in her life.

A stabbing pain came from her heart. "Just answer me. Yes, or no."

"Why do I get the feeling Sheila has something to do with this?"

Ashley sank into the nearest chair. "Yes, or no, Greg. That's all I'm asking."

"He told me he had one in college. Apparently it flared up again after you left him. He admitted that much to me because he was on the verge of a breakdown not knowing where you were. That's when I told him about City Creek's smokeout program. He grabbed for it like a lifeline."

"Has he smoked in front of you?"

"I know he has wanted to, but since I don't smoke, he has refrained from doing it around me."

She could hardly breathe. "So maybe he doesn't have a problem, and the clinic was simply a ruse to get the two of us together."

After a long silence, "If you can believe Sheila over your own husband who adores you, then I can see there is no hope of a reconciliation."

Her eyes closed tightly. It came down to whom Ashley believed.

The agony was starting all over again. If Sheila was telling the truth about Cord not having a smoking problem, then she was probably telling the truth about her pregnancy.

Clearing her throat Ashley ended with, "Thanks for talking to me, Greg."

"Wai—"

But she couldn't talk any longer and put the receiver back on the hook, thankful that Sister Bernice wasn't anywhere around. The head nun had probably gone outside to summon the children for lunch.

Ashley studied the card she'd unconsciously crumpled. *Dr. Robert Moore, OB GYN. The East Bench Clinic.*

She buried her face in her hands, wondering where to go from here. This was one time when she didn't feel like confiding in Sister

Bernice. Right now she didn't feel anyone could help her.

Never in her life had the urge to run and keep on running been as strong, but Sister Bernice's earlier admonition prevented her from bolting.

As Cord's wife, it's your duty to find out the truth.

But whose truth *was* the truth? Ashley's old fears were back, threatening the joy she'd been experiencing for the last few days. Sheila couldn't have manufactured that doctor's card. No doubt she truly was pregnant. All it would take was one phone call to find out.

I swear before God I've never slept with Sheila, Ashley. I'll take a lie detector test if I have to.

Oh, Cord. Has it come to that? A lie detector test?

Her heart shattered, Ashley left Sister Bernice's office to go to her room, all appetite having left her.

"Do you have to go home today, Ashley?" One of the little girls from Sunday school stopped her at the top of the stairs.

The word *home* reverberated in her mind. *Where was that?* With Cord?

"I do, Becky. But I'll come again."

"Promise? I like you."

"I like you, too, and I promise you'll see me again, darling." She gave the seven-year-old a big hug, then hurried off as fast as her pregnant body would allow.

Throughout the remainder of the afternoon, Ashley stayed in her room to finish the baby quilt, more often than not having to wipe her eyes so she could see to make stitches. There was no buffer against the agony brought on by Sheila's unprecedented visit to the orphanage.

Ashley found herself wishing she could stay at St. Anne's indefinitely. The thought of having to go home with Cord and live under the same roof with Sheila was tearing her to pieces. The possibility that he might have lied to her about his smoking problem had stolen the ground out from under her.

If Sheila hadn't lied, then how much of what Cord had said over the last few days could she honestly believe?

She felt like she was right back where they'd started last Monday morning. *Adversaries*. But with one difference…

This time Ashley was determined to see this thing through to the bitter end. Though she had no hope for a happy outcome, Vince had made her understand that she needed to resolve certain issues or she would continue to battle them long after the divorce was final. That idea was insupportable.

"Ashley?"

She looked up to see Sister Bernice in the doorway. The head nun had no idea that Cord's stepmother had been the woman who'd come to see her earlier in the day. Sheila would have used another name.

"Yes?"

As much as Ashley wanted to know the details of their conversation, she couldn't bring herself to ask any questions.

As far as she was concerned, she'd come to the end of the line. No one could help her except herself. What was it Sister Bernice had said a few days ago? "You're a big girl now, Ashley."

That's right, Sister. I'm on my own.

"Your husband has arrived and is waiting most impatiently down in the foyer," she imparted that little bit of news with a smile.

Ashley got up from the bed. "Thank you for telling me."

At her unemotional response the nun's keen eyes took on that familiar, quizzical look. Sometimes Ashley thought the older woman was a prophetess because she always knew when something was wrong.

"You've been a blessing in disguise here. I hope you haven't overdone it. Run along now. Don't keep him waiting."

"You're sure you don't need me for anything else?"

She darted Ashley a severe glance. "I can think of dozens of things, but not when you're pregnant and not when your place is with your husband. Courage, my dear."

It's going to take a lot more than that, Sister.

"Thank you for letting me stay here."

Sister Bernice knew Ashley too well. A vexed expression broke out on her face. "We're all indebted to you for the extra pair of hands, but now you must go. God bless you. Call me whenever you need me."

Ashley's throat swelled. "I will."

Before she broke down in front of her mentor, Ashley reached for her overnight bag. Cord had kept everything else with him.

After saying a little prayer for guidance, she made her way down to the foyer. Even from the distance his imposing presence made itself felt.

"Darling?" He fairly leaped up the first flight of stairs to meet her halfway. The next thing she knew, he'd swept her off her feet and carried her all the way out the front door and down the stairs to his Land Rover.

Heedless of who might be watching, his mouth plundered hers like a bridegroom eager to start the honeymoon. So deep was his euphoria, Ashley thought he couldn't tell that she wasn't participating as enthusiastically.

But he finally let her go, she felt his all-encompassing gaze. As it enveloped her, she noticed a sudden tightness around his mouth, a rigidity to his movements. A look of anguish mixed with pained confusion darkened his eyes.

"Ashley?" His voice throbbed with the question he hadn't asked yet.

She feared he was going to embrace her again. "Please don't kiss me anymore."

His head reared back as if she'd physically struck him.

"Let's just get in the car and go, Cord."

To her horror, his expression turned faintly satanic. "Two days ago we didn't know how we were going to live until we could be together again. Now you don't want me touching you. *What in God's name has Sheila done since I left you in the hospital parking lot?*"

Ashley would have answered him, but the sickness rising in her throat made it impossible. Misinterpreting her silence, he yanked the passenger door open and helped her inside.

Terrified of him in this mood because this latest development had sent him over the edge, Ashley avoided his murderous gaze as he slammed the door and went around to lever himself behind the wheel. After starting the motor, the tires fairly screeched as they drove away from the curb and entered the mainstream of traffic.

After passing through the next intersection, Cord suddenly veered into the left lane and turned into the parking lot of a supermarket. He drove as far away from the building as possible and found an isolated parking space.

They both sat there for a minute without saying anything. Then she heard a noise that sounded like ripping silk.

"All right. Start talking, Ashley. I want to hear everything from the beginning."

Without looking at him, she extended the hateful card which she'd put in the pocket of her maternity top.

He took it from her fingers. "What in the hell is this?"

"Sheila gave it to me when she came to the orphanage earlier today. She said that if you called her obstetrician at that number, he would answer all your questions."

Another minute went by in deadly silence. His quiet rage was more quelling than anything she'd ever known.

Taking a shuddering breath she said, "If you don't mind, I'm going to run inside the store for a few items."

"I *do* mind."

Ashley let go of the door handle, unwilling to cross him further at such a precarious moment.

"I *knew* I shouldn't have left you alone." His voice rasped. "The whole time I was gone, I had this gut-wrenching premonition something might go wrong.'' He jerked his head toward her. ''Don't shut me out. Not now, Ashley.'' She heard an underlying current of desperation behind the demand.

Staring at her hands she said, ''If I intended to do that, I would have disappeared from the orphanage and made certain no one could ever find me again.''

An unintelligible expletive escaped his lips. ''Undoubtedly she told you *I* was the father of her supposed baby.''

''She said she wasn't sure,'' Ashley muttered. ''Apparently she's been sleeping with another man, but they've always taken precautions. However since I'm pregnant with your child, she's pretty sure it's yours.

''I warned her that you would insist on a DNA test, but that didn't faze her because she wants to know the results as much as you do. It seems she and your father hoped to produce a new heir to the company since your heart wasn't with the business. But the accident that killed him ended their dreams to create a dynasty.''

As she talked, Cord's face hardened into an inscrutable mask. She would have stopped talking, but indescribable pain drove her to get it all said.

"Originally she planned to terminate her pregnancy. That's why she came to the hospital the other night, to talk to you about taking time off from the company to go into the hospital for the surgery.

"But when she discovered I was carrying your child, she changed her mind since it's more than probable she's pregnant with your child, too. Therefore she's planning to carry it full term. If it turns out that the baby isn't yours, she'll give it up. That's why she came to St. Anne's today—to discuss future plans for her child with Sister Bernice."

The dangerous quiet coming from his side of the car terrified her.

"And you bought every word of it…" came the gravelly sound at last. "So— The moment I leave you alone, Sheila plans another encounter and in a few seconds destroys everything you and I have achieved for the last week at the clinic."

The constricting bands around her chest made it difficult to breathe, yet she found the temerity to look straight into his eyes. "She said you made it up, that you didn't have a smoking problem.''

His glazed over. ''She really did a number on you, didn't she.''

''She told me to call Greg if I wanted to know the truth. H-he said he'd never actually seen you smoke.''

An oppressive darkness seemed to engulf him. ''Under the circumstances, I don't understand why you left the safety of the orphanage, let alone why you're sitting here with me.''

No person could fake the kind of desolation she heard in his voice. But at the same time, he wasn't attempting to defend himself.

''Neither do I,'' she blurted because of her pain. ''But our child has the right to know his father, and I'm too close to my due date to want to do anything to jeopardize his health or mine. So I'm going to stay with you.

''I'll even sleep in your bed and let you make love to me if that's what you want. There's so much infidelity in the world today, why should I expect anything different.'' She made a sound between a laugh and a cry. ''At least I know you'll always be kind to me, and a loving father to our child. What is it they say? It's better to take the hell you're sure of. Besides—''

''Don't say another word!'' he cut her off savagely.

''Why not?'' She kept it up as if he'd never spoken. ''You wanted an explanation for why I'm still sitting here. I'm simply trying to tell you all my reasons, one of them being a promise I made to Sister Bernice.''

''*What promise*?'' His complexion looked ashen.

''To find out for myself whose truth *is* the truth. A pretty formidable task.''

''*Ashley*—''

''I only have one more thing to say.'' She ignored his tortured imprecation. ''Because it will cost quite a bit to redecorate the house to accommodate two new babies, I guess I should deem myself fortunate that you're such a wealthy man. However, I want to make one thing clear.

''It doesn't matter to me where you and Sheila shop to outfit the nursery for the child that might be yours. Just remember that the furniture which is going to be delivered from Forsey's tomorrow is for the baby you fathered with *me*!''

Fury turned his eyes an inky blue. "Do you really think I would expect you to live in the same house with Sheila after what she's just said and done?"

Fire scorched Ashley's cheeks. "After such an elaborate strategy to get me to come back to you, do you really believe I would walk out on our little *ménage à trois* now? *Not on your life, Cord McKnight*! If it's going to go down, we'll all go together."

He sat there stone-faced. "No, Ashley. I can't let you do it."

"You don't have a choice," she lashed out. "Unless of course you know you're guilty and have decided the risk of exposure might be too great after all."

"I admit I'm worried," he muttered darkly. "After what you've just told me, I'm convinced Sheila is emotionally disturbed. Possibly dangerous."

Ashley let out another angry laugh. "That must be the stock excuse every man since Adam has thrown in a woman's face when he has run out of reasons to explain her.

"Let's face it, Cord— Sheila is nothing more than a grasping, self-serving female who has always had a thing for you. Maybe you've encouraged her. Maybe you haven't.

''Whatever the true explanation, she's willing to lie, cheat, distort, manipulate anything and anyone at hand to get what she wants, and she's terribly good at it. I give her credit. I really do.

''But you don't have to concern yourself about me. I've finally grown up. I confess it took me rather a long time. More than most, in fact. Chalk it up to my obscure beginnings.

''Needless to say, the blinders are off. I'm no longer the naive, insecure, pathetic little creature from the orphanage who can't fight her own battles. I'm capable of lasting as long as Sheila, if not longer.'' She took a deep breath. ''May we go home now? I'm hungry, I'm tired and I need to put my feet up.''

The ten-minute ride to Cord's family home was made in complete silence. Ashley realized she had been talking and acting totally out of character. Clearly Cord didn't want to take her home, but for the moment his fears for her emotional and physical comfort had overcome his worries about Sheila and any threat she represented.

Though Ashley hadn't planned to fling any of those words at Cord, evidently they had poured from her soul. In a way, they had laid the groundwork for the days ahead.

The only thing that could make Sheila angrier than to see Ashley walk through the front door of Cord's home, would be to have to live around his wife who no longer felt intimidated by the other woman's presence. Sheila wouldn't know how to handle the new Ashley who was accepting of the status quo. Who even *welcomed* it.

Her mouth curved at the corners, a reaction Cord noted with an oblique glance.

That would be insupportable to Sheila.

That would be Ashley's strategy from here on out.

"Hi!" Ashley shouted as they walked through the front door of his house moments later. "We're home. Sheila!"

As Cord followed her inside, the other woman appeared on the elegant staircase dressed in an apricot brocade robe that molded to her willowy body and brought out the sheen of her blond hair.

"I had no idea you'd be arriving this early."

That's right, Sheila. You didn't know which way the wind was going to blow.

"Cord got back sooner than expected." Ashley preempted anything her husband might have said. "And I was starving. I thought I'd order pizza with extra cheese and all the toppings. Do you want some with us?"

Ashley wished she had a camera so she could have captured the startled look on Sheila's face.

"No, thanks," she said in a tone of distaste. "I don't intend to put on any weight with this pregnancy that isn't absolutely necessary."

"Your morning sickness must be pretty bad to pass up pizza. I've got some medicine in one of my bags that will help. As soon as I've unpacked, Cord will bring you the bottle.

"All you have to do is take one pill every night and you feel great the next day as long as you eat some crackers and drink some Coke before you lift your head from the pillow. I swear it works like a charm. Darling?" She turned to Cord who was going along with her act, but she didn't miss the stunned expression coming from his eyes before they narrowed.

"I'm going upstairs and take a nice warm shower. Will you please bring the pizza when it comes? We can eat it in bed. I'll order Coke in case you want to join us for a little family get-together, Sheila. Our two favorite British sitcoms are going to be on TV in a while. We don't want to miss them.''

So saying, she hurried up the stairs, chugging past Sheila in the hope of reaching the next floor before she laughed hysterically in the older woman's shocked face.

But for that little show of bravado, Ashley ended up in Cord's bedroom out of breath and moaning over leg cramps that almost incapacitated her. When she finally got her second wind, she phoned for pizza.

With that important detail out of the way, she slipped out of her clothes and went into the ensuite bathroom to relax under the spray. To be able to act any way she wanted around his stepmother and not be nervous was so liberating, she could have squealed for joy. Not even the sight of Sheila's shampoo in the shower, or one of her see-through peignoirs hanging on the bathroom door hook had the power to shake her.

Ashley knew enough that if Cord were still intimately involved with Sheila—*if* he'd come home earlier today to be with her before showing up at St. Anne's—he still wouldn't have allowed Sheila to leave those items around for Ashley to discover.

The more she thought about it, the more Ashley wondered if Cord's stepmother wasn't just the slightest bit worried that nothing she'd done so far had driven him and Ashley apart.

"What are you up to now?"

While she'd been in the shower, either Cord's mood had improved somewhat or else she had imagined the trace of amused irony in his tone as she emerged from the bathroom in her white granny nightgown with the peignoir and shampoo in hand.

"Umm… I smell pizza." The aroma was coming from the box on the marble-topped double dresser.

Not batting an eye, she handed him the items, then rummaged around in her train case for a certain vial of pills. "Ah, here it is. Will you please see that Sheila gets this medicine along with her other things?" She lifted her gaze to his. "She must have forgotten to take her personal belongings with her."

A look of pained admiration flared in his eyes. The ache in her heart deepened and she wheeled away from him.

If he truly turned out to be the enemy, then heaven help her because he was loved and beloved, and there didn't seem to be anything she could do about it.

Refusing to entertain thoughts of Cord and Sheila together, Ashley ignored him by reaching for a large piece of pizza. She sensed rather than saw him finally leave the bedroom. As soon as he'd gone, she turned on thc TV and got under the covers.

It felt so good to lie down she couldn't believe it. Though hunger battled with fatigue, by the time she'd consumed the first slice, she was too tired to get up for a second piece. The last forty-eight hours at the orphanage had taken their toll.

At some point Cord finally came to bed but she was scarcely coherent. She heard him say Dan's name, but she only caught snatches of random words before she felt his lips brush her cheek and oblivion take over.

"It couldn't be nine-thirty!" she cried out the next morning when she awoke to an empty king-size bed. No telling how early Cord had gotten up.

He'd said something about Dan last night. Maybe they had agreed to meet early at the office.

She carefully worked herself out of bed, noticing that his green robe had fallen to the floor. Ashley pulled the nightgown over her head and deposited it on top of the robe. In a few minutes, she would gather up everything they'd brought home from the hospital and start a wash.

While she was in the bathroom freshening up and putting on a clean maternity outfit, the phone rang. Assuming she was alone in the house, Ashley moved as fast as she could to the bedside table to get it.

"Hello?"

"Ashley?" Her body always trembled at the sound of Cord's deep voice. "Did I waken you?"

"No. I was up." *Barely.*

"I called the furniture store and they'll be delivering the baby's things between twelve and three, so I'm going to come home at noon. Later on in the day we'll drive over to St. Anne's and get your car."

She blinked. "That's right. I forgot. It's still in the parking lot."

"I think we can both agree that last evening we had other things on our minds. In case you haven't been downstairs yet, I asked Katy to do some grocery shopping. You shouldn't have any trouble finding something good to eat."

As usual, Cord was thinking of Ashley's needs. *Talk about killing me with kindness.*

Unless his routine had changed, Katy was the cleaning lady who came in once a week and did odd jobs when occasion demanded.

She cleared her throat. "Thank you. I'm sure I'll be fine."

"Ashley—" He sounded anxious. "Don't ever hesitate to call me if you need anything. The entire staff has been alerted. They know to put you through to me no matter where I am or what I'm doing."

Her index finger curled around the phone line. "I'm not ready to have the baby yet, Cord. But I promise that when I start to experience the signs Dr. Noble told me about, you'll be the first one to know."

"I'm going to hold you to that," he vowed fiercely. "In the meantime, just be careful, darling." The endearment tugged at her emotions. So did the protective warning.

"I will."

"Good," came his response, eloquent with relief. "I'll see you in a couple of hours."

The line went dead.

Bemused by the mixture of gruff tenderness in his tone, she was slow to put the phone back on the hook and didn't readily respond to the knock on the door.

When it sounded again, she turned. "Is that you, Katy?"

"No. It's Sheila."

No wonder Cord was worried. His stepmother hadn't shown up for work yet. Bracing herself, she told the other woman to come in.

When Ashley saw what Sheila was staring at, she was glad she hadn't cleaned up the room yet. Cord had eaten the rest of the pizza. The empty carton plus a half-empty bottle of Coke were still on the dresser. The covers and pillows of the bed were in total disarray. To anyone looking, the clothes lying in a heap on the floor were mute evidence of a mutually satisfying night.

Normally Sheila was a cool, collected woman who put every one of her sex at a disadvantage. But this morning, Ashley could see pink blotches on her seemingly flawless skin and her gray eyes looked charged with a strange light.

In as pleasant a voice as she could muster Ashley asked, "Did you take a pill last night? Did it reduce your nausea?"

Sheila's head reared back. "You think you're so clever."

A strange calm had come over Ashley. This moment had been a long time in coming. "I've had a good role model in *you*."

Sheila's muffled gasp told Ashley she'd hit a nerve.

"You may be with Cord again, but you'll never be sure if he and I have been lovers."

The odd expression on her face, the unattractive twist of her mouth, took Ashley back to those early years at the orphanage when Marsha had baited her mercilessly for the sheer pleasure of watching Ashley suffer.

Marsha had been all bluff, but Ashley had been too naive and vulnerable to see through it. She'd been a child then. Now she was all grown up, and her vision had improved with age.

Pure revelation started flowing through her so hard and fast, she felt giddy. Like a fantastic gift, sure knowledge came to her.

Cord's truth *was* the truth!

"Do you know something, Sheila?" Her voice shook with a surfeit of emotion. "Not until this moment did I realize you're a total fraud. Thank God, Cord never gave up on me or our marriage. His love compelled me to come back here and face you.

"You've lost, Sheila. There's no more damage to be done. Give it up and try to live a decent life for the sake of your baby."

A mocking laugh flew out of her throat. "*I'm* not pregnant, you stupid little foundling."

Ashley shouldn't have been surprised, but she was... "Then that's another blessing I'm thankful for."

"Trust you to believe me," Sheila derided her. "I never saw anyone as gullible or naive in my life. It's been like taking candy from a baby."

Again she reminded Ashley of Marsha who constantly laughed at her own misdeeds—delighted in them even.

Lifting her head Ashley said, "Cord told me about the night many years ago when he was just a teenager and you invited him inside your apartment. He indicated that he'd left without sleeping with you, but you obviously couldn't take his rejection. That's why you've been trying to make him pay for it ever since, even to marrying his father and attempting to break up our marriage.

"Why don't you go someplace else where no one knows you? Cord's father left you plenty of money. He and I are going to be moving back to the Teton's after the baby is born. You can have the house. Sell it for a fabulous price. Do yourself a favor, Sheila. Resign from the company and start a different life elsewhere."

Her gray eyes glittered with an unholy light. "Maybe I will. Since Cord is going to be home at noon, I'll wait and discuss everything with him."

Ashley watched her leave the room, realizing that Sheila had listened in on her phone conversation with Cord earlier. It certainly hadn't been the first time.

Months ago Sheila had overheard Greg and Cord discussing the smokeout clinic. That was how she knew details only Cord would have known.

This is a game to her. All of it has been an elaborate, treacherous game.

Cord's right.

She's emotionally disturbed.

Like her husband, Ashley had the strongest premonition Sheila could be dangerous.

Lunchtime was too far away. On impulse she walked over to the phone and punched in Cord's number at the office. Without preamble she told the receptionist to get her husband immediately.

Seconds later, "Ashley? What's wrong?"

"I-it's Sheila. Come home *now*, Cord!"

She must have communicated her fear.

"I'm on my way."

Too jittery to stand still, Ashley made the bed and tidied the room. When she thought enough time had passed, she walked over to the window facing the street and watched for Cord's car.

Though Sheila's bedroom was just down the hall, the large, two-story traditional home swallowed sound. Ashley had no idea if Cord's stepmother was still upstairs or not, let alone what she might be up to.

The minutes dragged by. Finally she saw the Land Rover roar into the driveway. With her heart pounding out of control, she left the room and fled into the hall. There was no sign of the other woman as Ashley started down the stairs.

But when she reached the landing, she caught sight of Sheila's blond head. The older woman was a few steps ahead of her on the stairs, intent on reaching the elegant foyer.

Ashley could hear her husband calling to her. Then the front door flew open and Cord's powerful frame burst inside. He saw the two of them at the same time.

"Darling?" he cried out.

Sheila's hand went to the pocket of her jacket, filling Ashley with inexplicable dread.

"Look out, Cord!" she screamed at the top of her lungs.

In her haste to protect her husband, Ashley tripped on the next step and fell forward, hitting her head against the banister. She saw bright lights, then everything went dark.

CHAPTER TEN

THE mournful wail of a siren reached Ashley's ears and brought her awake. At first she thought it was farther away, until she opened her eyes and discovered she was riding inside an ambulance with a male paramedic leaning over her, taking her vital signs.

Her head hurt and she had low back pain with a kind of dragging sensation in her pelvis. All of a sudden she remembered everything.

"*Cord*!" she screamed and tried to move, but her head and neck were held in some kind of brace and the attendant cautioned her to lie still.

"I'm right here, darling," came the deep voice of her beloved husband who she could now tell was crouched near her feet.

Hot tears gushed from her eyes. "Are you all right? Sheila didn't hurt you? I thought she had a w-weapon of some kind."

"I'm fine," he said in a ragged whisper. "Don't worry about me. Sheila has gone out of our lives. All that is important is you and the baby.''

The mention of their unborn son reminded her that the pain in her back was starting to come all the way around to the front, and the pressure was building.

"Have I hurt the baby?'' she cried out in panic.

The attendant remained calm. ''You hit your head pretty hard, but fortunately for you, your husband caught you before you landed on that marble floor, so no bones are broken. Since you've come back to full consciousness and your vital signs are strong, the only thing serious to report is that the fall broke your water which means your baby is going to be born a little sooner than you expected.''

"Oh, no!''

"You're going to be fine, darling,'' Cord rushed to reassure her. ''Dr. Noble has been notified.''

She couldn't stop the tears. ''I—I was hoping he'd be born on your birthday. I wanted him to be my present to you.''

"Have you forgotten how much I love early birthday presents?'' he said huskily. ''Especially this one.''

"But we're not ready for him yet! I haven't bought any diapers or little shirts or sleepers or—"

"With one phone call I can have all those things delivered to the house. The only thing that matters is you."

"No. It's not!" Ashley half-sobbed, uncaring that the attendant was privy to their nightmare. "I've been horrible to you, Cord. How can you ever forgive me for not believing you?" Her voice rang out. "When Sheila came into the bedroom this morning and started baiting me again, I suddenly realized that she had lied, about *everything*!

"I'm such a wretched creature. You don't deserve to be married to a horrible wife like me."

"You're the only wife I want or need," he answered emotionally.

"I don't see how. I've been an ugly person on the inside for so long. Even Greg was shocked at how bitter and hard I had become. I hated myself for it, but—" Her voice trailed off as she began crying in earnest.

"Hush, darling. Sheila made victims out of everyone, starting with Dad. What we can be grateful for are true friends like Greg who encouraged us to never give up on our marriage."

"I know," Ashley moaned. "And Sister Bernice. They could both see what I couldn't see."

"What *we* couldn't see, Ashley," he amended with a residue of pain in his voice. "Sheila had even poor Dan hanging by a thread, slowly poisoning our relationship until he stopped believing in himself and me. But that's all over.

"Dan is going to run the company from here on out. As for you, Mrs. McKnight, we're going to have our baby and be a real family. Forever." His voice shook.

"Oh, Cord—" Those words brought her so much joy, she didn't stop sobbing until she felt the ambulance come to a stop.

"We're here, darling. It won't be long now."

"Don't leave me, Cord."

"As if I would."

The next few minutes went by in a blur as Ashley was taken to emergency to be examined. She had gone into labor but it was progressing slowly. Eventually they placed her on a gurney and sent her to the maternity floor.

Cord held her hand throughout the journey, his midnight-blue eyes never leaving hers.

"Feel like *déjà vu*?" he whispered when they put her in one of the labor rooms.

Her misty gaze feasted on his handsome features. "Was it only a week ago? It seems like we've lived a lifetime since I came to join you for the clinic."

"I know the feeling," he muttered thickly.

"Well, well—" a familiar voice broke in on them several hours later. "What have you been doing to yourself to get that goose egg on your forehead, Ashley?"

"*Dr. Noble—*"

He came over to Ashley's side, smiling down at her. "It's all right. I know all about the accident. You were given something to speed up your labor, but it hasn't worked. At this point I'd deem it advisable to perform a cesarean. Don't worry," he said when he saw her anxiety. "If another miracle occurs, you and Cord will be able to have a second and a third child without any problem."

Cord sucked in his breath. "That would be wonderful, but right now all I care about is Ashley." The wealth of love in his tone humbled her.

When she looked at her husband—how drawn and pale he'd become—she realized that the trauma of the last eight hours had finally caught up with him. *He was afraid for her.* She could see it, feel it.

Just then she experienced an outpouring of love for him that overwhelmed her entire being. Every step of the way he'd been so strong for her. Now he needed her strength.

"Sweetheart," she whispered, squeezing his hand. "I'm going to be fine. In a little while we're going to have that baby we've wanted. I'm so happy, I could burst!"

Her blue-green orbs were on fire for the love she had for him. No shadow of fear lurked as her generous mouth broke into a brilliant smile.

"*Ashley*—" he cried, covering her lips in a trembling kiss.

"As you can see, Cord, there's nothing to worry about," the doctor murmured. "Now, if you can relinquish your wife long enough for her to be prepped for surgery, I'll have an orderly find you a mask and gown so you can watch the delivery."

At Dr. Noble's words, Cord lifted his head. Excitement now warred with his anxiety.

"I'll see you in a few minutes," she whispered, feasting her eyes on his attractive face and powerful physique before he left the room with obvious reluctance.

"Okay, Ashley," the doctor said as soon as they were alone. "Let's go have a baby, shall we?"

"Yes!"

"Dr. Ball will administer the anesthetic. You'll be awake and feeling fine the whole time. You might experience a slightly dizzy sensation when I take the baby from your womb, but it will be over in seconds. I've already contacted your pediatrician, and she'll be in the delivery room with us. Any questions?"

"No," she answered with shaky excitement.

"When did you last eat or drink?"

"Nothing today. A piece of pizza last night, about nine."

"That's good news," he muttered while he examined her. "I find you in excellent shape for someone who took a nasty fall. Just relax now and let us take care of everything."

"All right."

"Between you and me—" he winked "—your husband is the one I'm concerned about. Being a brand-new father is a scary experience for us men, but especially for Cord who didn't think he would ever be one.''

''I know,'' came the shaky admission.

''Capable, protective men like your husband feel particularly helpless at a time like this. He's in awe of your strength. For the moment he has forgotten that you have a partnership with God. It gives you power beyond your mortal reserves. Every time I deliver a baby, *I'm* in awe of it.''

Ashley stared up at him. ''Thank you for being here for me.''

His eyes shone with sincerity. ''It's a privilege.''

Fifteen minutes later Ashley couldn't feel a thing from her chest down.

''Okay. Let's go.'' Two orderlies wheeled her out of the room and down the hall through the doors marked delivery. It was one of the strangest sensations in the world to be lifted onto the operating table and not be able to move her legs.

Everyone was in hospital green and masked. Dr. Noble talked happily with the nurses and Dr. Ball as Ashley was draped with sterile sheets, her feet placed in the stirrups.

She moved her head to the side and caught sight of her husband coming into the delivery room. The nurse indicated the chair he was to sit on. Ashley had an idea Dr. Noble had done that as a precautionary measure in case Cord felt faint. It made Ashley smile.

Though Cord resembled a doctor, his anxious dark blue eyes gave him away. They fastened on her and never left her face throughout the delivery.

While Dr. Ball constantly informed Ashley of what he was doing, Dr. Noble got started on his end. A few breathless minutes passed. Just before she was told she was going to be given a little oxygen, she heard a gurgle and Cord shot out of the chair.

"Oh, ho—" Dr. Noble made a satisfied sound as he lifted the baby. True to his words, Ashley felt a little dizzy and breathed deeply through the mask, but the sensation passed.

All of a sudden she saw her baby still bathed in amniotic fluid. Even so, his perfect little head was covered with Cord's dark hair. She started to cry for joy, mask and all.

"Have you two ever got a beautiful son! Come here, Cord, and take a look."

Her husband needed no urging. "*Ashley*—" Now his rapturous cry rang throughout the delivery room.

"He's looking good, breathing on his own." This from the pediatrician who'd taken the baby to examine him.

Excitement permeated the atmosphere.

"Your son is twenty-three inches long and weighs in at nine pounds four ounces. Being born three weeks earlier doesn't seem to have fazed this big guy at all."

"He's a whopper," Dr. Noble agreed with the pediatrician. "When you do a job, you really do it, Cord."

Ashley thought she knew what happiness was until the mask was removed, and her wiggly baby who made newborn noises and was wrapped in a blanket, was placed in the crook of her arm.

Her eyes raced from the curly dark hair to each adorable feature. "Cabe," she spoke to her little boy. "We're here. Your mommy and daddy are right here."

Cord's masked face was right next to hers. "We are, son."

Their baby's little eyes were looking at them as if he could really see them. It tugged at her heart and her soul quickly memorized every inch of him.

She marveled at his sturdy body with its broad shoulders, the tiny fingers with their square ends, the long feet and toes, visible testimony of the man who fathered him.

"Oh, Cord—I—I can't believe it. I just can't believe it." She broke down. "Cabe's here. He's *beautiful*."

"You're both beautiful." Cord was so choked up, he couldn't talk.

"We hate to break this up," Dr. Noble broke in, "but I need to finish taking care of Ashley. Cord, you can go down to the nursery with the baby. Your wife will be in recovery for a couple of hours, then she'll be taken to her room where you can join her."

Cord pulled off his mask, then lowered his head. "I love you," came the throbbing declaration against her lips, then he followed the nurse who was pushing the baby's cart out of the delivery room.

Dr. Noble patted her cheek gently. "I'm almost through here, Ashley. We've given you a hypo so you won't have any pain for a while. I'll be in to visit you in the morning."

Already Ashley could feel the effects of the drug. Her thank-you came out slurred as she sank into a state of ecstatic oblivion. Ecstatic because she would awaken to the husband and the brand-new son she adored.

It was after ten at night when the orderlies came to wheel Ashley from the recovery room to her private hospital room. Despite the fact that she'd just had surgery and her head throbbed where she'd hit it, she couldn't wait to see Cord and hold her baby again.

The first sight to greet her eyes was a vase of at least two dozen red roses. Cord's gift made her eyes fill. Then she saw another smaller floral arrangement of yellow roses and baby's breath which had been placed on the utility table. Something told her those were probably from Greg and Bonnie.

She looked around for Cord but there was no sign of him yet. Maybe it was just as well because she couldn't keep her eyes open.

The next time she awakened, it was mid-morning. When the day nurse came in and started taking care of her, Ashley asked for her purse so she could try and make herself look a little less hideous.

Just to brush her hair and put on lipstick helped her to feel a little more human. The nurse talked to her about breast-feeding her baby. While the fortyish woman was showing her how to get started, Ashley heard a noise in the hallway. There had to be at least a half dozen babies crying their heads off.

"Do you think one of those is mine?" she asked the nurse in an excited voice.

But she didn't hear the answer because Cord suddenly entered the room seeming larger than life and too handsome for Ashley to contain her emotions. "Cord, darling!"

His eyes looked burningly alive as he approached her bed. "If I hadn't been there to witness it all for myself, I wouldn't believe you've just had a baby."

She wanted to tell him exactly how he made her feel, but his lips smothered any sound as he engulfed her in a kiss that said so many things, she forgot where she was or what was happening. That is, until she heard a baby's lusty cry which was growing louder by the second.

"Our son is dying to see his mother," Cord whispered against her avid mouth. "Just don't forget that his father demands equal time with you later.''

''I'll never forget,'' she vowed, pressing another kiss to his lips before he backed away enough for the nurse to place Cabe in her arms.

''Oh—'' Ashley half-cried as she removed the folds of the receiving blanket. ''He's so beautiful, Cord. Look at him.''

''I've been down in the nursery with him the whole time, getting everything on video. They even let me bathe him this morning,'' her husband exclaimed with deep satisfaction. ''I'm now an expert.'' He pulled up a chair next to the bed.

''How wonderful! Did he love his bath?''

Cord's smile hurt it was so tender. ''He did.''

''Look at his ears and eyelashes. Aren't they adorable?''

Together they examined every inch of him, exclaiming, laughing with delight over every perfect part, especially the little faces he made.

Cord was quick to point out the likenesses to her, the telling details that proclaimed him their child and no one else's.

The baby quieted down, seemingly content to have both parents fussing over him.

"He's more mature than the other babies," Cord confided with fatherly pride. "I made it my business to find out that he's the biggest newborn in the nursery."

Ashley laughed. "No wonder I was so uncomfortable! But I'd do it all again for another one just like him." She kissed the soft skin of his cheeks. "He does seem solid, doesn't he? And gorgeous, just like his father," she cried out, still trying to believe that the miracle had happened.

"*Ashley*—" he whispered thickly. "I've wanted this for so long..." He caressed the side of her neck with his lips, unable to contain his emotions.

Despite the drug still in her system and her exhaustion, the sensations he aroused shot through her body like wildfire. She knew her hormones were raging right now, and Cord's nearness only made them that much more pronounced.

"So have I, darling," she said when she could find her voice. "Everyone in the world should experience this happiness."

Together they doted on their son until he started to show signs that he was hungry. At that point Ashley did her best to accommodate him.

The nurse explained it took time to do it right. In a few days it would all come naturally. Her optimism reduced some of Ashley's anxiety, especially when Cabe finally fell asleep satisfied.

"You're ready to pass out, too," Cord murmured. "I'll put him in the crib right here by your bed."

"Don't leave me," she begged him after the nurse had administered more painkiller. The IV was still in her hand and wouldn't come out till morning. Then she'd be able to eat.

"There's no chance of that!"

The primitive ring of those words sent her off to heavenly oblivion. When she awakened a couple of hours later, she discovered her husband in a lounging chair, the baby fast asleep against his shoulder, their cheeks touching.

Her heart turned completely over. If only she had a camera to preserve the moment!

Fortunately the nurse popped in before either of them awakened. In a whisper, Ashley prevailed on the older woman to hand her the video camera Cord had put on the dresser.

Though somewhat shaky, she took a minute's worth of video before handing it back to the nurse. That part of the film would be a priceless treasure.

To Ashley's chagrin, the nurse had to take the baby away to the nursery, but she promised to return with Cabe in a couple of hours.

Carefully, she eased him off Cord's broad shoulder, then settled him in the cart and left the room. If a person could die from too much happiness, then Ashley was a prime candidate.

She lay back against the pillows and watched her husband who had been through as much emotionally as she had. Not only the delivery of the baby, but the scene at the house which had precipitated Cabe's premature birth.

Sheila. The one dark shadow. Ashley needed to know exactly what had gone on with his stepmother. She wouldn't rest until he told her everything.

As if his mind had extrasensory perception, his eyelids opened and he sat up a trifle disoriented. ''Where's Cabe?''

''They took him back to the nursery a few minutes ago. I'm glad. You needed the rest.''

He levered himself from the chair and came over to the side of the bed, bestowing a long, lingering kiss on her mouth. "How are you feeling? Honestly."

"Sore, tired, strange and absolutely ecstatic."

Cord's expression sobered. He searched her features. "The goose egg is going down."

"That's good, but I probably have a huge purple bruise by now."

"We can thank providence that's all you have."

"Cord—tell me about Sheila, about what happened after I blacked out."

He stood up, rubbing the back of his neck absently. "When you called the office, Dan and I had just been talking about her, and her potential for evil. I heard the fear in your voice. That's when I told Dan to phone emergency and get an ambulance. To be honest, I've had an uneasy feeling since Sheila showed up at the orphanage. All the way home from the office I had this gut-wrenching fear that she might try to hurt you physically."

Ashley's breath caught. "I thought she had a gun and was going to kill you because she couldn't have you. Her hand was in her pocket. She looked so determined and just kept on walking downstairs toward you."

He shook his head. "She had the keys to your car in her hand."

"*My* car?"

"Yes. She showed them to me, insisting that she had just come down the stairs to wait for a taxi. She intended to go to the orphanage and bring your car home, as a favor to you.

"Naturally I didn't buy it and took the key ring from her. It's my belief that if she could have left the house without being seen, she would have taken a taxi there and then tampered with your car after bringing it home so the next time you ever drove it, you might get in some kind of accident."

"Oh, Cord."

"When she could see that I didn't believe her, she said she was leaving Salt Lake and wouldn't be coming back. I told her it was a good idea since the board had voted her out permanently of any position with the company.

"At that point, a taxi pulled up in front. No sooner had she gotten in it, than the ambulance arrived. All I could think about was you and our baby. It's my opinion she took Dad's money and ran with it. She'll never be around to hurt us or anyone else again."

Ashley let out a deep sigh. "That's the best news I ever heard."

"Darling?" He reached for her hand and kissed it. "Let's promise that we'll never look back again, never think about the pain of the past again."

She pulled him down to her.

"I'm way ahead of you, Cord. I just wish I were in a position to show you exactly how I feel about you. If you can just wait a little longer..."

"Is Sister Bernice feeling better? Can we see her for a minute?"

The receptionist looked up at Ashley and Cord who held their four-week-old baby in his arms. They'd learned that the nun had been down with the flu and that was why she hadn't been able to make a visit to the hospital when their baby was born.

Ashley was fully recovered from the surgery. When Cord suggested they take a drive in the fresh air and stop by to see the woman who had influenced Ashley's life for good, she thrilled to the idea.

"Sister Bernice is just fine now. I believe she's still in her office. Go ahead and knock."

Ashley felt Cord's arm tighten around her waist as he ushered her toward the far door.

"Come in."

Ashley turned the handle and they entered.

When she saw them, the nun beamed. "I was just thinking about you, and here you are with your precious child."

"We heard you had been ill, but this was the soonest we could come to see you. Cabe wants to meet you."

The nun extended her hands. "I've been just as anxious to meet him." Cord crossed the expanse and lowered the baby into her arms.

The sight of her husband with his little dark-haired replica brought a lump to Ashley's throat. That lump expanded as Sister Bernice kissed Cabe and spoke to him with all the tenderness of a loving mother.

As she put the baby to her shoulder and patted his back, unworried that he might burp on her scapula, she darted Ashley a loving glance. "Do you know you were only a month old when your mother brought you to St. Anne's, Ashley?

"You had a lot of hair, too. But you were tiny and suffered from colic. This robust son of yours is bursting with health and acts totally contented.''

''You haven't heard him when he's hungry. During the night he cries out for his mother and probably keeps the neighborhood awake.'' Cord grinned.

''Of course,'' she quipped. ''How else is he going to grow up to be tall and straight like his handsome father!''

Ashley's eyes shone like stars as she stared at her husband. ''Cord helps by getting up and bringing him to me. Half the time it's a fight to see who gets to hold him after he's been satisfied.''

Sister Bernice chuckled. ''You're a very lucky, very blessed little boy, Cabe.''

''We're the lucky ones,'' Cord interjected with emotion. ''I suggested to Ashley that we drop by today. She thinks we're here simply for a visit, but I had another motive, as well.''

The nun crossed the baby to her other shoulder, her look attentive as she waited to hear what he had to say. Ashley was no less curious.

''I don't know how much my wife has confided to you about me and my upbringing. Needless to say, I was born to wealth, but it didn't bring me a great deal of happiness. My real happiness began when I met Ashley.

"Therefore, I would be ungrateful if I didn't thank you for being the person you are, for always being there for her. You were the one who challenged her to fight for our marriage.

"Because she listened to your advice, we're back together and we're moving to the Tetons where I've accepted the position as chief ranger."

"Congratulations."

"Thank you. As my way of showing appreciation for all you've done, I've turned over the deed of my family home to St. Anne's, to use as you might see fit. My attorney will contact your people next week.

"It's very large, and has a big yard. Perhaps it could serve as a kind of halfway house for your older children who work part-time and go to college. Or maybe a place for children who are ill or handicapped. That will be entirely up to you. Except for a few personal mementos, I'm leaving all the furnishings as is. Ashley and I have no need of the home or the money. It will make me happy if I know it is being used for a worthy cause."

Ashley bowed her head, so touched by his generosity, so moved, she couldn't talk. Sister Bernice seemed to be having the same problem.

"I'm also setting up a fund to provide for its maintenance. St. Anne's will always have a special place in my heart. After all, it was Ashley's home."

The nun's eyes misted over. "Do you know that just the other day, we were informed that because the building doesn't meet the earthquake code, we have to find another place to temporarily house everyone. I have no idea if they'll raze the building and start over, or try to remodel it. You can't imagine what your gift would mean, especially coming right now."

Cord smiled. "I'm glad then."

Ashley couldn't wait any longer. She got out of the chair and threw her arms around Cord's neck, hugging him so hard she almost knocked him off the chair.

The nun stood up, still holding Cabe. "On behalf of St. Anne's, I'll accept your gift. On one condition."

Curious, Ashley's head swerved toward Sister Bernice.

"That you let me keep this little fellow for a couple of nights. I want to really get to know him, but I can't do that when parents as doting as you are around. Of course, it has occurred to me that the two of you could use some much needed private time together."

Cord's dark blue eyes darted Ashley a private message of desire that made her heart leap right out of her chest. Not only had they both been exhausted because the baby kept them up during the night. But they'd been following doctors orders which prohibited intimacy until her six weeks' checkup.

But for a fussy baby, the last few nights those orders would have been impossible to follow.

If they left Cabe with Sister Bernice now, Ashley knew exactly what would happen. So did Cord. In fact, his elation was so palpable, Sister Bernice secretly winked at Ashley who blushed a deep rose.

"We accept your condition," Cord spoke with unabashed eagerness. "If you need any-th—"

"I won't," the nun assured him with a satisfied smile. "We have everything your little boy could want right here, don't we? Say goodbye to your mommy and daddy, Cabe. Tell them to have a good time and not worry about you.''

Though Sister Bernice was the only person in the world besides Cord Ashley trusted with her baby, it was a wrench to leave him.

That is until they left the office and Ashley looked up at her husband. The love streaming from his eyes reminded her that it was time to dote on him for a change. This remarkable man who had never given up on her or their marriage.

Suddenly Ashley realized the moment had come to concentrate on this man, to renew her vows to love and adore him. Cabe had had a surfeit of attention. Now it was Cord's turn.

EPILOGUE

"Umm... I smell prime rib roast and potatoes au gratin cooking. What's the occasion, my love?"

Cord was home?

He'd come in much sooner than she'd expected. Because of the children, she still hadn't had a chance to bring out the candles with their best china and crystal yet.

Their three-year-old son, Cabe, and their adopted two-year-old, Ross, seated in their high chairs, cried out in delight as their daddy entered the kitchen.

He gave each of them a loving greeting, then made a beeline for her standing at the kitchen sink of the ranger's cabin and kissed the side of her neck.

She squealed. "Brr... It must be freezing out and it's only mid-September!"

"You know winter always comes early to the Park. We're going to get our first major snowfall tonight, so I headed back early. What

do you say we put the children to bed as soon
as possible and have a long night under the
covers all to ourselves.''

My thoughts exactly.

Out of breath with excitement, Ashley put
down the hand mixer she'd been using to whip
the cream for their fruit salad and turned in his
arms, eager to feel his mouth on hers. She
could never get enough of her husband.

After a day's deprivation, their mouths and
bodies fused in mutual need, but their noisy
little boys insisted on some attention, too. She
felt Cord's chuckle before he reluctantly let her
go and said he'd feed them while she finished
dinner.

''No, no—'' she blurted. ''I've given them
their food and they'll be ready for bed by the
time I have everything done for our dinner.
Tonight I want you to enjoy a hot bath and
relax. I'll call you when it's time to eat.''

His keen gaze played over her features.
''Why do I get the feeling something's going
on?''

She averted her eyes. ''Can't a wife do
something special for her husband once in a
while?''

Cord reached out to her once more, enfolding her in his arms. "You do special things to me and for me every day and night of the week. I'm the luckiest husband in the world. But tonight I sense something different about you."

"Well, you're just going to have to wait."

"You know I hate waiting for anything," he confessed without an ounce of shame before devouring her mouth.

"Did we win the lottery?" he prodded.

"We don't need to win the lottery." She chuckled, trying to get away from him. The children were becoming more raucous but Cord didn't seem to notice.

"Have your birth parents been trying to find you?"

"No, darling, nothing like that, and you know that's never mattered to me…"

"Did the adoption people ring? Are we getting the other baby we've been waiting for? Is that what this is all about?" By now he was smothering her with kisses.

"Not exactly."

Suddenly all his playfulness vanished. He stared down at her, his eyes intent, watchful.

She could never keep anything from him. Her breath caught in her throat as she whispered, "You think you can handle another miracle which should be arriving about eight months from now?"

Like a charge of energy, the green in those hazel depths ignited. His hands tightened in her hair. "I've already been given three miracles. The day you came back to me pregnant, and the day we adopted Ross. Is it possible a man could be so blessed as to have any more?"

She smiled. "This new baby I'm carrying is living proof."

He looked like a man with a marvelous secret before he turned to the boys. "Hey, guys? Did you hear that?"

Now that their father had spoken, they suddenly stopped making noises and stared at him.

"By spring things are definitely going to change around here. You're going to be joined by a new member of the family, Mary-Ashley."

"I hope it's a girl, too," Ashley murmured behind him. "But I'm afraid the gender of our babies will always be your department, darling."

As Cord turned back to her, the joy radiating from his countenance was a sight she would never forget.

"Let's get the little guys to bed, then climb into our own while we discuss boys' names, just in case. When we've decided on the right one, we'll celebrate with a midnight feast. How does that sound?"

Her heart was racing. "You grab Ross while I grab Cabe. I bet I'm in bed before you are!" she laughingly called out her challenge.

"Want to make a bet?"

She plucked Cabe from his seat and gave him a huge kiss on the neck. "Win or lose, I always win because I'm married to your daddy."

"Did you hear that, Ross?" Cord picked up their blond two-year-old and held him high in the air. "I think your mother said she loves me. *She loves me. She loves me*," he chanted as the four of them left the kitchen.

I love you, Cord McKnight. Never make any mistake about that. I love you.